'*The Beautiful Ones* captur
through the overpopulation
Faure weaves the interconne
the wealthy, environmenta
poverty, into a thriller that moves from today to 2081 and
lays clearly at the readers' feet a challenge for all of us to
change current behaviors now.'

> Paul Ehrlich, author of *The Population Bomb* and Bing
> Professor of Population Studies at Stanford University

'A tremendously ambitious, thought-provoking and worth-
while project. O. M. Faure has conjured up a colourful cast
of characters caught up in an entertaining story in which
action is informed by important ideas about our global past,
present and future. An impressive achievement!'

> Sue Belfrage, author of *Down to the River and Up to the Trees*

'*The Beautiful Ones* is a story that people need to read and a
discussion that needs to happen in society. The characters
feel like they're alive. The book made me laugh out loud a
lot... and it also made me tear up. I would keep the clapping
going for a great story with a compelling idea and a gripping
narrative.'

> Tony King, author of *Fishing for Music* and Australian
> Songwriter of the Year 2009

'Captivating, unsettling, bold. O. M. Faure's *The Beautiful
Ones* isn't afraid to hit you hard with the "first they came for
them and now they're coming for you". With such authen-

ticity and heart, this trilogy will touch your life and spark many conversations.'

Isabelle Felix, author of *Deafinitely*

'In *The Beautiful Ones*, O.M. Faure offers us a chilling glance into a world not so very far from our own, and paints a compelling picture of a dystopian future that may be closer than we think.'

Clare Kane, author of *Dragons in Shallow Waters*.

ALSO BY O. M. FAURE

THE CASSANDRA PROGRAMME SERIES:

The Disappearance (prequel)

THE BEAUTIFUL ONES (TRILOGY):

Book 1: Chosen

Book 2: Torn

Book 3: United

CHOSEN

BOOK 1 OF THE BEAUTIFUL ONES TRILOGY

O. M. FAURE

FORWARD MOTION PUBLISHING, LTD.

ISBN: 978-1-9164370-1-2

Published by Forward Motion Publishing, Ltd.

Cover design by Stuart Bache of Books Covered & Micaela Alcaino | Cover
images © Shutterstock

If you would like to know more about the sources and data, please consult the bibliography at the end of this book. A list of book club topics will also be provided to readers who subscribe to the newsletter.

Visit www.omfaure.com to join the conversation today.

For my godfather and mentor Alastair Pugh (1928–2019).
At his side, flying became possible.

'Anyone who believes in indefinite growth on a physically finite planet is either mad, or an economist.'
— Sir David Attenborough

CHOSEN

PROLOGUE

Poolesville, Maryland, USA, December 1970

ALASTAIR PARKED the mustard-coloured Mercury Comet and looked up at the large red barn. It seemed vaguely forbidding, in the eerie silence of the snowy landscape, looming in the twilight of this long, tiring day.

The car made small 'pling, twing' sounds as it cooled down. Alastair sighed, not looking forwards to this meeting. He'd left this visit for last, as he didn't like giving bad news. But he could hardly prolong his trip any more. It was nearly Christmas and he needed to go back to London, to be with Vanessa for the birth of their first child.

He wrapped himself tightly in his fashionable camel coat, regretting once again his choice of clothes. He always forgot that the US had worse winters. He stepped out gingerly into the slush, picking his way to the barn door.

The smell was, as always, overpowering: piss and fermented faeces, the decay of cadavers and the odour of thousands of small bodies.

'Ah. There you are, Sagewright.'

'Good evening, Professor. Sorry I'm late. You know... the weather.'

Calhoun waved away Alastair's apologies, as if dispersing a cloud of smoke. He signalled for the young man to follow him to his office.

They passed by a blue, square box about one hundred inches wide and sixty inches high; and Alastair, holding his breath, sneaked a peek over the edge.

Hundreds of mice were milling around a complicated set of tunnels and nests, arranged like rays from a central sundial.

'How many left?'

'About a thousand,' the Professor said with a pronounced Tennessee twang.

'Only?'

Calhoun harrumphed and held the door to his office open while he waited for the young man to enter. Alastair suddenly felt preposterous with his long sideburns and his tight trousers flaring at the ankles. The old Professor must think him a ridiculous young fop, who thought he could tell him how to run this experiment.

Inside the cramped office, Alastair shifted stacks of papers from a chair and sat down. Calhoun was already sitting behind his desk, his light blue overalls spotted with mud. He pulled a bottle of whisky and two disgusting-looking glasses from a drawer. With a wave of his chin, he put the question silently and Alastair accepted with a nod. Words sometimes seemed superfluous after nearly three years.

'So it's happening again, I take it?'

The whisky burned in Alastair's throat and he started feeling warmer almost immediately. He relaxed and leaned back in the orange chenille chair.

'Mmh. Yes, all four phases: Strive, Exploit, Stagnation and Death.'

'They can't have already transitioned into Death, surely?' Alastair asked, aghast. Calhoun threw a frustrated look at him.

'Of course they have, they always do,' he said gruffly.

'But I thought that, for sure, this time... I mean we created an environment that was ideal, a mice utopia... Did we make a mistake? Were all the conditions respected?'

'Yes, of course, boy! Who do you think I am? The box was escape-proof; the temperature was maintained between seventy and ninety degrees Fahrenheit; the mice had all the water, food and nesting material they could possibly need. No predators, of course, and they were all selected for their excellent health.'

'How did they do this time?'

'Well, as usual, their numbers exploded exponentially, doubling every fifty-five days until they reached their ideal population size: six hundred and twenty. That's when the shit started to hit the fan, as it always does.'

The young man winced at the American's profanity. But whereas Alastair was just starting out his career as a venture capitalist for scientists, the professor was respected and much older than him, so he smiled politely and listened.

Calhoun pulled out a pipe and stuffed it with grimy fingers. His salt-and-pepper hair was too long at the back and he needed a shave. He pulled a few puffs from the pipe and smoothed his moustache reflexively a couple of times.

'What I don't understand is why the experiment always

fails. From day three hundred and fifteen to day five hundred and sixty, they doubled in numbers only every one hundred and forty-five days, but all the behavioural sinks started happening again as they neared the two thousand individuals mark.'

'Like last time? The widespread aggression among males and females alike?'

'Yes, exactly like all the twenty-four times before this experiment. Vicious attacks.' The old man looked even older all of a sudden. 'The fathers stopped defending the nest and left. The mothers, left on their own, became aggressive and started filling traditionally male roles. Then it worsened and mothers abandoned their young; the rearing and weaning period was cut short, and sometimes the females even ate their young.'

Alastair felt bile rising in his throat and swallowed.

Calhoun sighed, took a gulp of his drink and poured himself another glass. He pointed the bottle's neck towards Alastair, who shook his head, thinking of the road ahead, probably dark by now.

'In the Stagnation phase,' Calhoun explained, 'the young don't receive the nurturing necessary to achieve proper emotional development. So when these young come of age, they try to form normal relationships with the other sex, but they're always interrupted by other mice, because of the overpopulated conditions.'

Alastair suddenly thought of the young disenfranchised populations of London but pushed the thought away. They were only experimenting on mice here. There was no reason to believe that humans would react in the same way.

Calhoun continued, rubbing his face despondently. 'By now, in Stagnation, the young don't enjoy social interaction because it's fragmented and unfulfilling. So they don't know how to court, how to parent, how to fight correctly.'

'I see,' Alastair said cautiously. Although, to be honest, he was not at all sure that he saw anything besides the broken old man before him, who wouldn't make him any money at all. He stole a glance at his watch.

'After the Stagnation phase, they entered the Death phase.'

'But I simply don't understand why, Calhoun. How come they die? Are you sure it's not from disease?'

'No, of course not. In the Death phase, they just stop mating, stop interacting, stop caring about each other at all. They grow old and die out.'

'How do you know when you're about to start the die-off phase?' Alastair asked.

'A group appears; there are just a few of them at first. They withdraw from all social interaction. They position themselves in isolated places and watch the rest of the over-crowded population fight each other for resources.'

'Well, that sounds sensible to me.'

'It ain't, son. Withdrawal from all social interaction means they're mentally deficient. They just spend their time eating, drinking, sleeping and grooming themselves. No sex, no interest at all in social interaction. They're broken.'

'What do you mean?'

Calhoun shrugged. 'Even when we took a few antisocial specimens from the Death phase and put them in another less congested environment, with female mice that hadn't been in the overcrowded space, they didn't know how to be normal anymore.'

'What do you mean, normal?'

'They displayed no social skills whatsoever. They just

continued to take care only of themselves and groom themselves obsessively until they died.'

'What do you think it all means?'

'That humanity is doomed.'

Alastair, who had been debating having another drink,
looked up from his empty glass in surprise.

'How do you mean?'

'I think it's like the Book of Revelation said...'

Alastair groaned internally and tuned out as Calhoun
launched into a convoluted metaphor about the four
horsemen of the Apocalypse. The poor man had dedicated
his entire life to this failed experiment. Complete population annihilation every time. No wonder that he was losing
his marbles and turning to the Bible.

'... So you see, mankind is exactly like these mice.'
Calhoun counted on his fingers and held out his thumb.
'One: we live on a planet that is inescapable and that has
finite space. Two,' he said, extending his forefinger, 'we have
food and water in abundance for all. Three: we'll soon eradicate all diseases. And four: we no longer have any predators. By my calculations, we'll hit the beginning of the
Stagnation phase very soon.'

'And then what?' Alastair asked, suddenly worried about
his unborn child.

'Then, like the mice, son, at first it will look like the
fertility rates per couple are dropping but the total population will continue increasing.'

'So what are you saying?'

'I'm saying that when we reach seven billion, we'll hit
the Stagnation phase and behavioural sinks will start to
manifest.'

'What? Aggression and all that?'

'Yes, exactly. And even worse, son, I estimate that the next stage will start when we reach fifteen billion.'

'What you mean the Death phase and inevitable extinction?'

'Yes, son, exactly.'

Alastair laughed. 'Fifteen billion! That's science-fiction, Calhoun. Don't be ridiculous. We'll never reach such an unthinkable number! We'll be fine.'

Calhoun reached for the bottle again, thought better of it and grabbed Alastair's forearm instead. Alastair glanced at Calhoun's grimy fingers on the sleeve of his Savile Row blazer.

'Don't you understand?' said Calhoun. 'I've tried twenty-five times. Twenty-five! Nothing can stop the progression.'

'Are you sure?'

'Yes, of course I'm sure! That's why I can't sleep anymore! As soon as we enter the Stagnation phase, it's the point of no return: humanity is finished.'

'So do you mean to say that once we reach seven billion, we'll be doomed, there'll be nothing we can do?'

Calhoun hesitated. 'Well... if we could infuse the young with a sense of purpose, maybe. Give them something to do, somewhere to go...'

'Where? There's only Earth, that's our own universe twenty-five enclosure, our own mice utopia; there's no escaping it, we're out of predators and there're already too many of us.'

'Maybe space exploration... I don't know, son, I don't know anymore.'

'Well, all that seems very unlikely to me.' Alastair chuckled uncomfortably. 'I can't believe we'd behave like your mice. We're much brighter than they are, for one.'

Calhoun looked at the younger man, his eyebrows

raised. He opened his mouth then pressed his lips together, shaking his head.

ALASTAIR DROVE BACK CAREFULLY in the snow, his headlights barely lighting the road. Fat snowflakes swirled in the beams of light. He couldn't shake a deep sense of unease following this latest meeting with the Professor. Towards the end of it, he'd had to deliver the bad news that he wouldn't be funding the experiment anymore. Alastair just couldn't see any way to commercialise the findings.

As they'd walked out of the lab, Calhoun had stopped to show him something. Alastair held a handkerchief to his nose and looked distastefully at the enclosure. Scarred, maimed mice were swarming at the bottom of it, heaped on top of each other. They were dirty, smelly and smeared with faecal matter. The animals walked all over each other, snapping at each other, in the overpopulated pen. While he was watching, a one-eyed mouse attacked another and ripped its tail right off. Disgusting creatures. Alastair had glanced again at his watch, anxious to get back on the road.

'See the mice there?' Calhoun said, pointing to a group of twenty or so white rodents, which had retreated to the higher levels of the cage. Their coats were shiny and immaculate, their demeanour calm.

'Those?' Alastair asked. He thought they looked much better than the wounded, dirty ones who were fighting for space below, all covered in scabs, scars and filth.

Calhoun tapped his pipe against the side of the enclosure. 'Yes, these. They're the deeply impaired ones who spend their time eating, sleeping and who care only about themselves. They're incapable of normal social interaction and lead the way for their species' extinction.'

'Oh.' Pity, Alastair thought. They *looked* alright. But they were the harbingers of doom apparently. By now he was eager to leave and catch his plane back home. He asked distractedly, 'And what do you call these?'

Calhoun smiled sadly. 'The Beautiful Ones.'

1

OLIVIA

L ondon, United Kingdom, May 2016

'*Ipsa scientia potestas est, igitur sapiens qui prospicit.*'
The Latin motto loops around a gold crest, gleaming against the cream paper, like an incantation, melodious and jarringly alien: 'Knowledge is power, therefore the wise look ahead.' Surrounded by cryptic symbols, a pyramid is embossed in the centre of the sigil. It winks in and out, and seems to radiate as the afternoon light plays with its triangular edges.

When I received the letter, my interest was piqued. I mean who writes letters anymore? Much less to invite someone to an interview.

Sitting in reception, palms getting clammy, I wait, discreetly flapping my right hand and willing it to dry before I need to shake anyone's hand.

The Mulberry Bayswater handbag waits patiently by my

feet, a remnant of a time pre-IVF when I spent my disposable income on things that made me happy instead of needles and hormones. Good job the patina it acquires with age is considered desirable, because it's old but still pretty, in a reliable, unglamorous way. Hopefully so am I.

This is definitely not your average law firm. Sunlight pours in through sash windows as pink cherubim and fat-bummed women in various states of undress glare down at me from the seven-metre-high ceiling. The circular reception area smells of wood wax and old money. It's quite impressive, truth be told.

'Who knows?' says the little singsong voice inside my head. 'Everything might turn out OK.'

A very nice coffee machine and a biscuit selection are beckoning from the rosewood sideboard, so, stuffing the letter in my handbag, I get up to have a look. I'm dressed up in my best stewardess impression: navy suit, frizzy red hair more or less under control and sensible pumps. My heels echo as I walk on the intricately decorated tiles. The posh receptionist looks up and dismisses me as inconsequential.

I've just made myself a tea when an impeccably dressed woman in her sixties approaches me. Her hair is tied in a bun and she's wearing patent stilettos, a pair of black pleated trousers and a bronze silk blouse with a statement necklace. I know better than to mistake her for a PA. Everything about her speaks of power.

I can tell she's sized me up in one glance. With a tightening of her mouth, she extends her hand.

Struggling to balance the teacup and saucer, handbag and coat, I manage to return the handshake without dropping anything. Good thing I'm on a diet or I'd have had to contend with a spoon as well. Silver lining of not remembering the taste of sugar, I guess. Oh who am I kidding; there is no silver lining when you give up sugar.

'Welcome, Olivia.'

That's odd, she sounds like she knows me. I search her face and something chimes in the back of my mind. Do I know her? I'm pretty sure I don't, so I go with the I-don't-know-you-from-Eve greeting.

'Hello, nice to meet you.' Oh gosh, I sound too chirpy.

'Yes, I'm sure.' She narrows her eyes and seems to hesitate to say something, then thinks better of it. 'If you'll follow me.'

She heads off at a brisk pace. Argh. What do I do with the tea? Obviously, drink it really quickly, scald my palate, then leave the cup and saucer on the sideboard. Drop my trench coat on the floor for good measure, lose my Oyster card. Fumble to pick everything up and quickly trot behind her before she realises I'm a dolt. Although, to be honest, it might be too late for that.

And breathe. 'Everything is all right, this is a no-stress interview,' the annoying singsong voice says in my head. 'You don't actually need this job.' OK, time to look like a credible candidate.

She opens the door with a pin code and a full handprint. Blimey, I've only ever seen a similar set-up once and it was at a very, *very* nice law firm. A thick cream carpet has replaced the antique mosaic tiles. The hallway is lined with closed doors, each with its own keypad. Bouquets arranged like modern art are positioned on antique consoles at regular intervals. Everything speaks in hushed tones of wealth, confidentiality and professionalism. I can totally do this.

Finally we arrive in front of the right door and my guide goes straight in without knocking. I was right then, not a PA.

There are three people already in the room, I expected

fewer. The grey-haired woman joins them and points me to a seat opposite them. Brilliant. Now I feel like a contestant on *Britain's Got Talent*.

'Welcome, thank you for coming today,' says a kind-looking man in his late forties. His slightly haphazard haircut can't hide that his ears are sticking out. 'My name's Andrew Catterwall. I believe you've met my colleague Theodora McArthur, who accompanied you here.'

Another man speaks up with a pronounced American accent. 'I'm Agent Nigel Critchlow.' He's in his late fifties, with an underbite and grey hair in a crew cut. His calculating eyes follow me behind thick, black, fifties-style glasses. 'And this is Aileen Foley.' He points to a slender woman in her early thirties who smiles.

'Thank you for inviting me. May I ask how you heard about me?'

'We've been following your career, Olivia, and felt you'd be a good match for our organisation,' Andrew answers.

I was expecting him to say that someone I work with recommended me. But what did he say? They've been following my career?

'I see.' I try not to sound too surprised. 'May I ask what sort of law firm you are?'

Now it's their turn to look slightly taken aback. Critchlow laughs, not a nice sound. I get the sense he's one of those people who laughs instead of saying something aggressive. His teeth are protruding and crooked. Is it possible to dislike someone within five minutes of meeting them? Well, it just happened, so I guess it is.

'There seems to be a misunderstanding, Miss Sagewright; we're not a law firm at all.'

Now that I think about it, my research yielded a surprisingly low amount of information. With such secrecy levels, I assumed they were a very exclusive firm, who valued their clients' privacy and worked through word-of-mouth. Who else would invite me for an interview? I have been working in law firms for the last fifteen years. Crikey, this is all very intriguing.

'Before we disclose any more, let's proceed with the interview. If we conclude that we'd like you to come for a second round, we'll ask you to sign a non-disclosure agreement and will inform you on a need-to-know basis from that point on.'

Need to... who do they think they are, MI5? Oh my God, maybe that's who they are. OK, earth to Olivia: focus. If I want to know more, I need to ace this interview.

Andrew Catterwall runs a hand through his hair, tousling it, and starts asking me the usual questions: achievements, relevant experience, strengths and weaknesses, etc.

As far as interviews go, I think this one goes well. I didn't have to force my round self into a square hole; I didn't have to pretend to be interested in the job – I really am interested.

I'VE TAKEN my Friday afternoon off for the interview and now I burst out of there, exhilarated. Not another boring job! Amazing, I can't wait to know more.

Tonight we should celebrate. I stop on my way home to pick up a few ingredients and a bottle of bubbly. Maybe tonight's the night. We haven't made love in so long.

'Hello?' I call as I push the front door open, my hands full of grocery bags, keys, handbag, umbrella, the works.

No answer. The rattle of machine guns echoes through the dark house, followed by high-pitched swearing.

'Kill him, kill him! Oh no, he's behind you! Too late – I'm dead.'

'Hello, Bear, I'm home!' I lug my load to the kitchen counter, turning on the lights as I go. As I unpack the spinach, the leeks and chicken, Martin doesn't even glance over at me from the sofa. Apparently, he can't stop playing; there's no 'pause' button for online games.

I sigh and start cooking, banging pots and pans about perhaps slightly louder than necessary. When the pie comes out of the oven, the little passive-aggressive dance begins, like every evening.

'Martin, it's ready.' I look longingly at his beautiful profile, hoping he'll turn his head. He still doesn't.

'I'm not done.'

'It's ready *now*,' I say, careful to lace a smile through my words.

'I can't, I have to finish this game.'

'How long will it take, Bear?'

'I don't know. It could be five minutes or thirty.'

'Please come eat.' I say, hating the pleading note in my voice.

'I'm not hungry anyway, I had a protein shake before you arrived and I'm going to the gym after this.'

Martin has decided that he's not 'a system-person', meaning that he's a free spirit. Last month, I encouraged him to quit his job. It just broke my heart to see him so miserable. Forced to keep business hours and dress in clothes that he hates. It's his fourth resignation in the last six months, but I'm sure he'll find something that he enjoys doing. Soon.

I can't very well blame him for playing *Call of Duty* with his brother, I mean what else is he going to do with his days? He doesn't really read. Maybe I shouldn't be so hard on him.

He did make a huge sacrifice by leaving Malta to come live with me in London. He hates it so much here. It was to be expected that he'd have trouble fitting in, what with all the hard-nosed and ambitious people in this city. This just isn't his forte. I ought to be more supportive.

I start to tell him about my interview but his eyes are on the door and he's zipping up his jacket. I don't do a very good job of explaining. Anyway, a few minutes later, he's off.

Biting my lower lip, I walk back to the kitchen, put a slice of pie on a plate and arrange the salad so it looks pretty. Nigel Slater would be proud, it's perfect.

'Sure, Martin, go to the gym,' I say to no one in particular as I sit at the dining table and light a candle. I'll save the prosecco for later. I shouldn't drink and there's no point in celebrating alone, I guess. I rub my left ovary and wince.

Only a month left to wait until the egg collection.

Dishes washed, I turn off the lights and shadows stalk me up the stairs to the dark, cold bedroom. My cat weaves herself around my ankles, as I inject the hormones, whispering a prayer for good measure.

I'm so close to my dream that I could touch it. I'm visualising my baby on a beach, his blond curls shining in the sun as I run my fingers through his hair. My son's delighted laughter skims and bounces above the waves like music.

I'm stubbornly imagining that Martin will be a good father, even though he farts and burps on purpose to annoy me, doesn't have a penny to his name and only wears sports vests, while I love opera, books and afternoon cream teas served in silver teapots at old-fashioned hotels. Yes, he'll be great. Our child, Max, will be beautiful and as soon as he's born, Martin will change his mind about having children, as all men do.

2

DEANN

B altimore, Maryland, USA, May 2016

THE MACHINE EMITS a pulsating high-pitched noise. My toes are cold and I feel out of place. How did this happen again? That's right, I'm being spontaneous, I scoff.

Normally, by the second round of an interview process I'd know everything about the hospital interviewing me. I'd know their mission statement, I'd have read their annual report cover to cover and I'd have networked my way into some insider knowledge.

'Alright, that's it, perfect. Now please hold still.'

The nurse positions a white plastic helmet over my head and fixes it, so it holds me down. Cozy.

But the usual interview prep is yielding next to nothing; I looked up the four people who interviewed me last month in New York and either those were pseudonyms or they've erased nearly all traces of their existence online. Theodora

McArthur used to be a Professor of Physics at MIT. Nigel Critchlow seems to crop up on military websites, but even when I search for cached versions, I can't locate his name anywhere. Andrew Catterwall worked in venture capital financing for London banks, but about twenty years ago he dropped out of the market and his profile shows nothing since then. Aileen Foley graduated from MIT at age fifteen with a double degree in computer science and engineering, and after that... disappeared as well.

'This is a functional MRI.' The nurse bends over me, as I lie trapped in the contraption's grip. 'We're going to take approximately fifty transverse-cut photographs of your brain while we monitor you. This will tell us how you think and where this activity takes place.'

She places a pump in my left hand and tells me to press it if I want to stop. In my right hand, she inserts a yellow pad with four buttons and positions my fingers on them.

'Press this when applicable, but don't move your head, DeAnn.'

She's fiddles with a mirror above my head, angling it so that it's level with my eyes and allows me to see a screen.

The table starts to drag me head first into the machine. I'm not great with confined spaces, so I breathe in and close my eyes.

'Alright, DeAnn, how are you doing?' Her disembodied voice is coming from inside the machine.

Fucking awesome, what do you think? 'I'm OK.'

'You're doing great, DeAnn.'

I wish she'd stop using my first name. I know what she's doing, she's trying to create a connection and make me comfortable, but I'm a doctor so I just find it irritating and condescending.

I flinch as the machine starts to clank loudly around me.

'We're now going to project questions on a screen. Choose the answer to the question by pressing the buttons in your right hand. Do you understand, DeAnn?'

'Yes.'

I choose between twenty dollars today or forty dollars in two days. Between going to vote or helping a person who needs an ambulance. Between colors, foods, people. The list goes on and on.

Then, finally, the clanging stops and the table creaks slowly out of the circular opening.

I dress and she walks me back to the waiting room where I spend the next hour wondering why I decided to interview for this position as I flip through magazines.

'Ms. CARPENTER?' A short, round Middle Eastern man is looking at me. 'I'm Doctor Farouk, please come with me.'

He takes off and I follow him to his office.

'So you're applying for a position with the Programme?'

Finally, someone who seems to know something.

'Yes, do you interview a lot of candidates?'

'No, it's quite rare for me to be called upon by the Programme. Baltimore's slightly out of the beaten path but I used to work with them in London, so they've asked me to screen a handful of candidates in the last fifteen years.'

'Do you know what the Programme is? What positions they are interviewing for?'

'I can't discuss that, unfortunately. Please have a seat.' He indicates a chair and closes the door. 'We were really impressed with your career to date.' He consults his notes. 'You're a geneticist at the Johns Hopkins McKusick-Nathans Institute of Genetic Medicine, correct?'

I could do the interview in my sleep. Where do you see

yourself in five years, what would you do in this situation, credentials and referrals, blah blah blah. I'm disappointed actually. After all the initial mystery, this is gearing up to be just another job at a major hospital. Dealing with patients, run of the mill diseases, nothing interesting to sink my teeth into.

Just as my interest is starting to flag, the doctor says: 'We're looking for certain functional connectivity patterns in the candidates. Only the ones who present with the right indicators can be allowed to erm... can be selected. We conducted a functional MRI and a diffusion tensor imaging scan on several potential candidates for field positions.'

He turns the computer monitor toward me, displaying two scans side by side. 'Could you please analyze the differences between these two MRI scans?'

I spot the issues immediately. The pattern looks just like a rare genetic disease that I have seen a couple of times in fetuses fathered by older men.

'You can clearly see here, the increased activation in the anterior cingulate cortex, the brain network that governs attention, coupled with reduced firing of inhibitory neurons,' I say. He looks pleased, so I continue, 'I assume that here on the left is a control test subject's scan and on the right is an abnormal scan.' The one on the right is lit up in yellow, oranges and reds in slightly different places.

Then I notice actual physical differences. The brain on the right is definitely larger... and is that? It can't be. Extra folds. I've never seen this before. 'There seems to be an atrophy in the subject's trapezius or sternocleidomastoid muscle and that could perhaps have led to expansion of their head size?' I check his face, unsure.

He nods, observing me. 'Could you extrapolate as to

what the result of this anatomical change might do to the subject?'

I narrow my eyes and grab his mouse, zooming in on the area. 'There.' I point with the cursor. 'A clear expansion of the fusiform gyrus.' Scrambling to recall my med school training, I say, 'So the subject will probably exhibit better pattern recognition, more intelligence, more connectivity.' I lean back against the back of my chair. 'It's subtle but the pattern is definitely there.'

His stubby fingers are joined in a steeple under his chin. 'Does this pattern fit a specific condition?'

'Not that I can recognize. But it resembles a genetically abnormal pattern I have seen before. So, probably steer clear of the candidate on the right.' I laugh.

'Actually, Ms. Carpenter, you misunderstand, these *are* the qualities we're looking for in our candidates. We require them to have that particular abnormality; otherwise, they cannot be selected.'

That's just fucking great, what a waste of my time. There's no way I'm going to spend the next few years of my career poking around the brains of 'special people'. I look at my watch and think of how to turn down this post politely, when he says something interesting.

'We have found out the hard way that we can only send certain people on missions. All field agents must have this specific brain configuration in their sternocleidomastoid muscle and the extra folds in the fusiform gyrus.'

'What happens to the ones who don't?'

'The process damages their brain.' His face twists in a grimace of distaste. I guess he's seen it happen and it's not pretty.

'You mean they suffer long-term consequences?'

'Yes, very much so. The technology mangles their minds.

They spend the remainder of their lives in bed restraints with no control over their bladders, or their sphincters for that matter. As you can imagine, the Programme is very keen to avoid this outcome and started including the MRI in the recruitment process a few years ago.

'Oh and by the way,' he continues, 'this means that if you ever wanted to become a field agent, you'd be eligible. But we're probably getting ahead of ourselves, here.' He chuckles. 'You're just here to apply for a position on the medical team, aren't you?'

'I'm sorry, what?'

'Oh yes, didn't I mention? The scan on the right is your own, Ms. Carpenter.'

My stomach drops. That's just not possible.

He sees my face and backtracks. 'You didn't know?'

I shake my head. 'Why would you look for abnormal candidates for this job?'

He frowns. 'This isn't an abnormality, it's in fact an incredible evolution of your brain and it opens a door for you to a new world of possibilities...' He stops mid-sentence and checks himself. 'I'm afraid I can't say any more at the moment. I'm sorry.'

'But I—'

He interrupts me, getting to his feet. 'So thank you for your time today. If all goes well, we'll meet again, Ms. Carpenter.'

He walks around his desk to stand in front of me as I get up, towering over him. He takes my hand in both of his. 'I was very impressed with your qualifications. I'm sure we'll meet again soon.' And with a smile he walks me to the door of his office and I find myself out in the corridor, aghast.

3

OLIVIA

L ondon, United Kingdom, June 2016

I'M LYING on a hospital table, legs akimbo, a penis-shaped camera rummaging in my vagina. The nurse is speaking to my business end about Brexit. She talks very earnestly to my pubes about how she'll vote to leave the EU. She's currently extolling the virtues of Boris Johnson, who she believes is acting in the best interests of our country. But really he's a hapless idiot and Brexit would be a monumental mistake. He doesn't stand a chance anyway. We're far too sensible a people to vote Leave.

The nurse is in her late fifties, she's the kind of thin person who's dried up and shrivelled like a dehydrated apple. Her office is wallpapered with photos of her dead dog (I asked). She spends her days talking to the vaginas of desperate, middle-aged women embarked on a journey that in most cases has less than a 10 per cent chance of success.

I'd start to talk about politics and books and general stuff as well if I were her. I mean, she's no different than a cabbie really; another customer every ten minutes, in and out, done and dusted. For her, this is a normal day; no pressure, no stress. Shoot the breeze, next client – and *voilà*.

Meanwhile for me this is a Hail Mary pass. My money, my hope, my health are all spent. This all-important scan will reveal if the treatment has produced enough follicles to go into egg retrieval, the next step. If there is only one follicle or if the drugs have not worked, all my hopes will splatter like a suicidal jumper reaching the pavement.

This has to work; I want to hear that my womb has obeyed my panicked commands, that God has listened to my fervent prayers, that Life has been swayed by my positive meditations. Instead I'm hearing about Boris Johnson, the dishevelled moron. Happy days.

'All is well,' she finally condescends to let me know. 'We can proceed to egg retrieval.'

How fantastic!

On go the blue cap and slippers as I change into the hospital gown, clutching the open back to conceal my nakedness.

This nurse is not so bad, really, dead dog and all. I mean, I've had worse.

For example, the cute Greek doctor who all the online-forum women swooned over; he checked his texts and ignored me while I waited silently for him to be done, sitting at his desk, an arm's length away. Or the crazy acupuncturist who was supposed to be the best in London but had her wig on askew and wanted £300 for ten bags of magic fertility tea. It smelled and tasted so bad that her receptionist recommended I drink it with a straw while pinching my nose shut.

I practically know by heart all the books about positive

thinking and attracting what you want. So I think happy thoughts, as I lie down on the trolley bed.

But still, doubt creeps in, through a chink in my positivity armour. I've left it too late. Forty-one. The years and probabilities of success are slipping away. My insides are old and my pipes are rusty. After all the IUIs, IVFs and ICSIs, this twelfth try will be my last.

The hospital bed rattles into the operating theatre, where the medical team greets me with kindness perhaps mixed with pity; they all know me by now. They put me under and proceed to puncture my ovaries to suck out the precious eggs.

A few hours later, groggy, bleeding and nauseous, I pull my pants, my trousers and my dignity back on.

Outside, torrential rain greets me, but I couldn't care less. I float inside the familiar bubble of hope and denial, whispering to myself in a singsong voice,

'This time it will work!' My left ovary whimpers with pain but I just press down on it and think positive thoughts.

4

DEANN

Baltimore, Maryland, USA, June 2016

'You fucking evil bitch!'

'Please watch your language or I'm going to have to ask you to leave.' I don't think the nurse, what's her face, will help. She looks down at some paperwork with a smirk and pretends to be busy.

'My language! My language? You just told me my child has a genetic condition as if it were an inconvenience interfering with your busy day. How about you learn some fucking bedside manners!'

The blonde woman is hysterical. At least her husband has the good grace to look embarrassed. He has one hand on her wrist and is staring at the screen where the deficient fetus is floating, oblivious, in its black and white amniotic fluid.

She shakes him off angrily and continues to shout emotional nonsense.

I tune her out and turn to the nurse. 'Call security.' Now she can no longer ignore me.

I am not responsible for this patient's poor genetic stock, her choice to settle down with an older man and her decision to leave it too late to have kids. I don't care really. This is nothing to do with me. I just gave her the news.

The day worsens when the Dean calls me into his office to demand I take a sensitivity class. It's hard not to snort.

'I really don't think I need to.'

'Did I say you *should* take the class? I meant that you *must*, DeAnn.'

'Look, Jeff, I don't really have time for—'

'When you came to me a few years ago, looking for a place on my team, I warned you that you'd have to work outside the lab and interact with patients regularly. You agreed.'

Today is making me regret that choice in spades. I'm much better with test tubes and petri dishes. People are incomprehensible.

He leans forward on his desk. 'Do you know how many people would kill to have your position? You can't have our benefactors thrown out by security for God's sake.'

I've been silent for a while, so he lays it on thicker. 'It's your second strike, DeAnn. There will not be a third. Do you understand?'

I nod, gritting my teeth. Why do I even put up with this? That mysterious Programme is looking more appealing by the day.

'OK, that'll be all.'

ALL THE HISTRIONICS and the drama have exhausted me and I am now winding down by working away on a pet project of mine for a few hours. The lab's hubbub recedes little by little as everyone leaves for the evening and I can finally hear myself think. I'm deeply immersed in my research when my phone beeps.

It's Trevor; I completely forgot that we have plans tonight. I hurry to the restaurant, drop my car keys with the valet and make my way to our table. As soon as I'm seated, his hand reaches for mine, before I have time to remove it. Looking at my fawn-colored fingers trapped under his dark brown hand, I wonder why I've always been attracted to dark-skinned guys; maybe so I can add richer color to my mix. Trevor, with his tall, toned body, shaved head and business-like demeanor, is perfect in theory. His corporate job's not great, but I make do with his MBA-level intelligence.

I don't know why the media harps on about women's ticking clocks. Men are the same or worse. All my male friends hit thirty-five and started asking their girlfriends to marry and have kids. It was like a fucking epidemic.

We used to rent small yachts and spend days at sea. Now I can barely get them to a bar on a Saturday night. They all have bags under their eyes and the only topic they seem capable of talking about is their progeny. It's worse when I visit; then their little monsters get their sticky hands all over my clothes and draw on my shoes in the hallway while I chat with their disheveled mothers in living rooms that look like war zones.

Trevor, by contrast, was cautious. He was older and made it clear he was interested in a relationship but not kids. Fine by me.

I liked that he kept to himself, that he didn't chase me all the time, that he wasn't head over heels for me. I could maintain my space, continue to live in my own condo, see him when I wanted sex. It was perfect for about two years.

Then things started to go south.

Last Sunday we went to have tea (tea!) at his parents' place and I got the distinct impression I was being discreetly vetted. His mother even eyed my hips at one point, for child-bearing purposes, presumably.

After a little Bible reading, some of the kids put on a recital. Relatives all sat around watching their offspring sing with 'oohs' and 'aahs'. So fucking wholesome I could have puked. My hands were literally itching to grab the Black-berry out of my Prada to check on work emails. But I behaved.

On the way back, Trevor was quiet.

So here we are, a few days after that God-awful family reunion; I've only had one glass of wine so far because he doesn't drink and I moderate myself around him.

Thankfully after fifteen minutes of awkward silence and stilted how-was-your-day-honey, our friends make their entrance. Philip's tall, blond and lanky with a permanent three-day beard. His eyes are hungry, his teeth too sharp, his handshakes too long. Philip gives me a one-armed hug, his hand sliding under my shirt and along the small of my back, sowing goosebumps in its wake. I readjust my blouse and kiss Carla on the cheek as I sit back down. She and I used to work together.

I don't think they'll last the year. They have two kids and she wants a third. Philip would rather stab himself in the eye. He texted me a couple of times over the last few months. His messages always appear benign at first, but between the lines...

A few weeks ago, Philip came by my place to vent about his marriage. We opened a bottle of Syrah and talked until late on the balcony, overlooking the bay.

Things got complicated pretty fast after we opened the second bottle in the kitchen. His hands found their way into my bra, mine frantically unfastened his belt. Then the over-powering hunger bit and nothing could have stopped us as we ripped each other's clothes off and he took me hard, on the kitchen counter. He looked hungry and mean.

He hasn't called me since, which I simultaneously resent and am grateful for.

Someone puts a hand on my shoulder, I flinch but it's only Jordan. I get up and he hugs me; a full-on, friendly, comforting embrace. He smells of fresh laundry and some-thing else as well, something pleasant. Two steps away, his girlfriend, Aliyah, is looking like she's just bitten into a lemon. Her black skin seems even darker against the too-short, bright yellow dress that hugs her thin, muscular body, stopping mid-thigh. The tips of her long black hair sway against her waist as she flicks it with her long, red, pointy nails. She always makes me think of a panther, ready to pounce and kill. But not before she has fun with her prey – and that would be poor Jordan right now.

Jordan and I met a long time ago. He had just returned from the Gulf War where he'd earned a scholarship. We met on the first day of med school. He teaches in Boston now and we have dinner every once in a while, when he's in town. He's pussywhipped but happy enough as far as I can tell. Of course, Aliyah hates my guts.

Jordan sits next to me and asks me how I am. For some reason I actually tell him about the MRI and the upcoming London interview. His head is cocked toward me, elbow on the table, full lips resting against his right hand. The wine brings the words more easily to the surface, as I look into his eyes and see understanding there, empathy and acceptance.

Aliyah laughs loudly at something Philip said and the spell breaks. Jordan puts a hand on her bare knee and starts a conversation with Philip. Soon they're immersed in their pissing contest about who has the fastest, most expensive, most obnoxious car.

The meal ends; it was good but I have my reservations about the place making it to Michelin-star status. Everybody else likes it. I guess I have high standards. We all wait for the valet, ignoring the homeless man on the sidewalk. I can't believe they allow them here. That's just not right. I should complain to the management. I'll write them later.

Back home, Trevor starts to touch me and I wish I'd had more wine because the sex is particularly bland tonight. I haven't told him but actually I like more spice in my sex life. He just isn't the type to oblige.

Soon, he's humping me in the missionary position, eyes closed, avoiding eye contact. His dark, muscular body is slick with sweat and the veins in his throat are bulging. Soon now; I repress a yawn.

It's definitely time to cut him loose. I move my hips a little faster and moan, running my nails along his back, digging in ever so slightly. That should do it. A big raspy groan and he's finally come.

He flops over next to me, cursorily pets my arm and gets up immediately to wash himself. Trevor doesn't do body fluids. I used to like that about him: he was always so clean. It appealed to the doctor in me, I suppose. I didn't realize that it also came with a side of compulsive showering before and after sex and no kissing after blowjobs.

'Was it good for you as well?' he says, as he walks back from the shower.

'Mmh?' I ask, checking my Blackberry.

He lies down and turns off the lamp on his side.

'Did you come?'

Well, it's too late to wonder about that, Trevor. 'Uhu.'

'Good night then.'

'Good night.'

THE NEXT MORNING, I wake up at 5 a.m. and go to the gym, as I've been doing every morning since 2005. I figured that if Condoleezza Rice could do it, then so could I. The gym part, not the Secretary of State part.

I come back an hour and a half later, and get ready for work. Finally, about five minutes before I have to go, I look in on Trevor in my bedroom. He's getting back into yesterday's clothes.

'Trevor, I'm leaving.'

'Have a good day.'

'No, I mean, it's over. I'm leaving you.'

He's hopping on one foot, pants around his ankles, pulling them up. Maybe I should have chosen a better time to do this. Hindsight twenty-twenty.

'What? Can we talk about this?' He stumbles, flails and catches himself on the side of the bed.

'Not now, I need to leave for work.'

There's a crestfallen look on his face. I guess his wholesome upbringing only prepared him for soft, malleable women who would have jumped at the opportunity to marry him.

'I'll call you later,' he manages.

'I'd rather you didn't. But you can if you have to.'

He finishes dressing and leaves the condo with me. There is an awkward moment when he starts to kiss me goodbye, out of habit, then stops.

Thankfully, it's over in a few minutes and he drives away as I get into my BMW. It was definitely the right decision.

5

OLIVIA

L *ondon, United Kingdom, July 2016*

I CLUTCH the banister of the scenic lift and suck my breath in as St Paul's white and grey cupola comes into view. It's incredibly close.

'Oh.'

Aileen Foley looks up from her clipboard. 'Yes, it's quite beautiful, isn't it?'

The 'second round' was surprising, to say the least. I couldn't believe it when they said it would be a medical. I mean I know I'm healthy, given the amount of tests I've done in the last four years of IVF, but surely having a blooming MRI was a bit much just for a job, wasn't it? At least it dispelled any notion that it might be a law firm position, as I can't imagine any lawyers caring about my brain configuration.

When the much-anticipated cream paper letter with the

gold crest appeared in my letterbox a few days ago, inviting me to the third round, I swept Bubblesqueak up in my arms and twirled around the kitchen in my pyjamas, singing 'Climb Every Mountain' while she clung on for dear life, meowing piteously.

We get out on the last floor and Aileen leads me to a conference room overlooking the city. A huge mirror reflects the view, giving the impression that we're surrounded by the city's rooftops. I tear my gaze away from the windows to look at the twenty or so people clustered in small groups around the room, and realise with a chill that these strangers are my competition.

Tea bags and mugs are set out in a corner, so I walk over to stand there and observe the candidates quietly. A man wearing a pinstriped blue suit that's too tight is talking loudly, making a woman laugh. His cufflinks are garish and his trousers slightly too short. He's bulging out of his shirt collar and his hair is stiff with gel. He looks down at the girl, hunching slightly to get close to her.

She's on the plump side but wears it more confidently than I do. Her dyed blonde hair is straightened and split on either side of her neck, dangling past her large breasts, making her look like a basset hound. Her orange-coloured arms protrude from a sleeveless dress, as she tiptoes on vertiginous platform heels. Obviously, she's also got bubblegum pink gel nails. Mmmh. These two seem made for each other. They turn to look at me and she laughs at something he whispers in her ear with a smirk.

A striking, statuesque, light-skinned black woman is checking her Blackberry, her thumbs flying on the small keyboard. I glance at her beautiful profile, feeling completely inadequate. She's at least five foot nine and wears a pair of impeccably-cut black trousers with a simple white blouse and a statement monochrome necklace. Her black pumps are elegant but sensible and her long hair cascades down her back in a shiny, straight style. She radiates authority, charisma and power.

She puts away her Blackberry and turns from the window to accept a cup of coffee from a blond hunk. Her 'thank you' has an American twang to it. The buff guy is the sort who can't lower his arms completely because of the size of his biceps. He speaks to her in confidential tones, his hands clasped behind his back, legs shoulder-width apart.

His eyes roam, as if making a note of the escape routes and evaluating each of the participants' physical strengths. His gaze slides over me like I'm not even here. I guess I haven't made it into his competitor assessment top ten, then. Maybe it's the fact that I'm wearing pink. Unless he has X-ray vision and can detect cellulite through my tights and skirt. Oh, get a grip, Olivia, I admonish myself, before I risk breaking into a fit of giggles. That would be catastrophic, given the company I'm keeping. All these people obviously take themselves much more seriously than I do.

Sitting at one of the tables, a tall, dark-haired Indian man is deep in conversation with a round, short black man. The tall man's ankle bounces slightly up and down on his knee despite his hand being clasped around it.

Opposite him, leaning forwards in earnest conversation, the black man with the full cheeks is explaining something, his hand gestures forceful. He's wearing crocodile shoes that seem too long for his feet. His suit is very good quality but his body is so rotund that it doesn't make much difference. His tie is shiny and a gold tie bar with a small cut stone clips it to his shirt.

Others are dotted around the conference area, mostly looking like professional soldiers.

At another table by herself, a woman sits deep in her own thoughts, pencil in hand as she sings to herself in Japanese and jots down notes in a small notebook. Her hair forms a curtain on each side of her face every time she bends over her work.

A large, freckled woman waddles over and offers the quiet one a cup of tea. The overweight woman sits down, raising her elbows to position her cup and saucer above her large belly, and starts to talk right away, barely drawing breath between sentences. Her daydreaming counterpart seems quite taken aback; I gather she didn't ask for a tea and has no idea why she's being lectured.

'You shouldn't sit here by yourself, you're supposed to show that you're a team player, I'm sure that's what they're looking for, you know. Once I interviewed for another position and...' the freckled woman goes on and on.

A tall, pale woman enters the room, wearing black from head to toe, her long brown hair tied in a plait. She scans the room and walks over immediately to Aileen, moving like a predator. The mousey admin girl looks startled at first and then placating as the striking woman speaks with intensity but in a voice too low to hear.

Spotting a stack of brown paper envelopes on a table at the back of the room, I stroll over to have a look. There seems to be one envelope for each person present and just as I spot the one with my name on it, the buff guy swings by, a mug of coffee in his hand. Under cover of chatting with me, he touches the floor-length mirror next to us. He glances at his reflection, then crosses his arms, and, taking a sip of coffee, surveys the room.

'What are you doing?' I whisper.

'Just a small test.' He sounds Scandinavian. 'It's a two-way mirror.'

His eyes dart to the entrance.

The chatter dies down and all gazes turn to Andrew Catterwall, who has come into the room and is standing next to Aileen.

'Welcome, everyone. Let's get started with our third round of interviews, shall we?'

My Scandinavian neighbour speaks up. 'When will we know what we're applying for?'

'This is on a need-to-know basis, Björn. You'll be briefed if you're selected.'

'There are twenty of us here, can you at least give us an idea of how many positions we're competing for?' the African man asks.

'Sorry, I can't, Woody. But what I can say is that you were part of a pool of one hundred candidates and only eight of you will move on to the next stage today.'

Different expressions etch themselves on the candidates' faces: arrogant, determined, absent-minded, attentive.

'If there are no more questions, let's get started.'

Andrew claps his hands together, rubs them together in happy anticipation and puts them on his hips.

'Right, everyone grab a folder from the table behind me. You have an hour to go through the file's contents. When the hour is done, we'll ask you to present your recommendations to a panel of judges. This is an individual exercise, so please do not work together.'

Aileen goes through our midst and collects our mobile phones in metallic plastic pouches, which she seals. Then she and Andrew wish us good luck and close the door behind them.

We all look at each other and, with a shrug, I pick up the envelope that bears my name. We sit at the chrome and glass tables and the room falls silent, as we become absorbed in our files. Mine contains newspaper clippings from 1909, describing the discovery of an oil field in Turkmenistan, followed by its exploitation. There are grainy pictures of a wellhead erupting in black rain. I rummage through the file and find a glossy magazine article from the fifties about Iran at the height of the Shah's reign. Little girls in tutus and Western-garbed women look incongruous in light of what happened to their country in the years to come.

There are photocopies of a homemade conspiracy-theory rag, with eyewitness accounts of various events in mountain ranges and forests with names I don't recognise. On my table, I spread out old photos, historical and topographic maps of small areas in the eastern part of Europe and the Middle East, and articles about border skirmishes and armed conflicts. It all seems unrelated. Recent medical articles describe research conducted on a population and a test group to detect autoimmune conditions; there's an estate agent's analysis of water quality and some balance sheets for a local refinery. Other articles recount the construction of a pipeline by the Soviets.

At first I struggle to make anything of this jumble of information. It just seems to be a random collection of material. I'm starting to get stressed as the hour slips away. I wipe my palms on the side of my skirt and take a deep breath. I'm not the only one who's anxious. The bovine-looking man in his City pinstripe suit seems less than impressed with his file. If his is anything like mine, then I bet he's wishing it contained financials and annual reports. He could probably interpret those in his sleep. The African-American woman, oblivious to her surroundings, is calmly making neat little piles of paper clippings.

Woody takes a long glance at his neighbour's pad and

starts writing furiously. I press my lips together and look down again, thinking about who might be observing us behind the mirror.

I chew on the end of my pen and stare at my watch. I only have about ten minutes left and I have no idea what I'm going to say to the interviewers. Something is nagging at me, though. I wish I had a map of the region. Frustrated, I grope inside the envelope and sure enough, it's there. Feeling like a dolt, I get the large map out and unfold it. And that's when it hits me: these articles are all linked.

The Soviet Empire used to occupy Turkmenistan, where the oil was found and which has a border with Iran. The pipeline originated in Russia but it crossed several borders. Remembering the articles about border skirmishes and conflicts, I trace the pipeline's route with a marker pen and reach the town where the medical research was done about autoimmune diseases. A picture starts to emerge in my mind about what is really going on here. Andrew comes back into the room and announces that time is up. I haven't had time to prepare a presentation but a narrative is forming that explains all of it, like a red thread linking the file's elements together.

Each of us is guided to a separate interview room. It takes me twenty minutes to paint a picture of what happened from 1909 to today for my two interviewers. I pin the map to a white board and use it as the backdrop to my presentation, producing each article chronologically, as supporting evidence for my narrative and use a marker to annotate the map and draw the links between each article, photo and event. Once I'm done, the interviewers thank me and, without further comment, invite me to return to the main room.

Pinstripe East Ender and his Towie Barbie are already

there when I get back. Woody is sweating profusely and wiping his forehead with a handkerchief. The Japanese woman is also back early and sits absentmindedly staring out of the window, as we all trickle in.

Aileen joins us and announces that we'll have a one-hour break as she points us to a trolley of sandwiches and drinks, so we all tuck in. I make a point of talking to everyone. The daydreaming woman, Yuriko, is a visiting scholar and is quite excited about meeting Theodora McArthur. Chatting to the Japanese candidate, I realise that the Professor's actually more accomplished than I thought and her achievements in the field of quantum physics are mind-numbingly impressive.

The tall, seemingly self-confident Indian guy is an IT engineer who's not entirely sure what he's doing here. But whatever this job is, he assures me he'll compete to succeed.

Woody has joined us from Switzerland where he works at the United Nations. He tells me funny stories about meeting famous politicians. I'm probably imagining it but I think he steals glances from time to time at me as if he thought I were credible competition. His smiles and jokes are tinged with a sort of anxious envy.

The pinstriped guy, Frank and his lady friend, Marjorie, are nowhere to be found and the African-American woman, whose name I learnt is DeAnn, is sitting in a corner typing furiously on her Blackberry. I'm about to bite into an egg sandwich when the freckled woman walks over with a plate piled high and starts to talk to me about what I should do about hydrating my hair and how she knows a great product I should use. She's annoyingly condescending but actually I completely need to know this.

Björn returns a few minutes before the end of the break, looking sweaty and bearing a protein shaker; he inspects the sandwich trolley but doesn't take anything. Instead, he sits in a corner, feet on a chair, and looks out of the window into the distance as he drinks big gulps of the vile-looking liquid. Andika, the intense woman in black, is standing alone in a corner, observing everyone.

Frank and Marjorie come back a good ten minutes late and both look flushed and slightly tousled. Maybe they went to a park for lunch, didn't see the time and had to run back. It's a fairly nice day outside, for a change.

A few minutes later, Aileen walks in, this time accompanied by Agent Critchlow, who explains the next stage.

'We're now going to take you through a more interactive exercise. This is a war game. You're each going to be given a role and you need to accomplish two things: first, behave as if you were really the person in your brief, and second, ensure that you learn as much as you can about the other players' objectives. At the end of the game we'll evaluate you on these two variables: whether you reached your character's target and how much information you gathered about the system and its stakeholders.'

Oh great! The nerd in me is delighted at the prospect of a role-play. I have elf ears and a full-blown Arwen costume at home and I love to indulge in the odd renaissance fair now and then so this is fun for me. However, some of the others seem slightly taken aback and less than happy.

Aileen spreads out paper envelopes on a table again and gives us thirty minutes to read our brief. The memo explains that there's a war brewing and we're heads of state, trying to take advantage of the situation for our respective countries. I'm the President of North Korea and my objective is to build up my country's nuclear capabilities while avoiding detection and sanctions. My secondary goal is to try to form a regional alliance with Asian countries despite our political differences.

I spend an enjoyable hour and a half running from one person to the other, negotiating to obtain uranium from Russia's black market, poaching nuclear scientists from France, pledging my innocence in front of the US President and generally having a ball. I'm such a do-gooder that playing a rogue statesman is sort of fun and liberating.

I observe all my counterparts and notice when they lie; I make notes of the deals they're happy to give me and the ones they refuse. The engineer is quite stiff and never negotiates; his default position is to give nothing and ask for everything. Woody double-crosses a couple of participants, but only DeAnn seems to realise and I hear her call him out on it. Frank bullies his way through the exercise with white-knuckled handshakes and unreasonable demands. Yuriko gives in to nearly every demand and looks increasingly tired. DeAnn does really well, maintaining her professional demeanour and negotiating calmly and efficiently.

By the end of the game, I have a pretty good handle of each candidate's hidden agenda and negotiating skills. We all get together for a final meeting, playacting a UN session and manage to avert a world war. After this, each of us is again called into a separate room and asked to list the other participants' strengths and weaknesses, describe flaws in their personalities and chinks in their strategies, as well as what we've surmised from their briefs. I write furiously, shaking my wrist at intervals to loosen it up as I try to remember what I saw and what was said, while making connections between the statements, looks and handshakes I've witnessed. It's so much fun. At length, having written all of it down, I go back to the main room and notice, surprised, that I'm the last one back.

Björn looks at me curiously, no longer dismissing me. Woody comes by and slides a hand behind my back, walking me to a side of the room. He asks me charmingly what I wrote about for so long. Andika, the intense panther-like woman, narrows her eyes and observes me.

Uncomfortable with the attention, I escape to the loo and while I'm there, manage to do my IVF injection. My thoughts return as always to my embryo, floating in frozen slumber in one of the hospital's cryogenic vats. My mind pokes at the image like a tongue unable to stay away from a sore. Soon now, loneliness will end for both of us. Soon both our lives will thaw.

I'd rather nobody knew about it, so instead of binning the empty syringe, I put it back in its box and hide the whole thing in my Mulberry. Then, smoothing my skirt, I walk back to the room, thinking everyone can see right through me and will guess what I did in the loo.

But as I push the glass door open, the Japanese scholar collapses on the floor, writhing, her mouth opening and closing, lips turning blue. Her frantic jerking has scattered the tables and chairs. Everyone in the room is frozen, still holding their mugs, standing around her.

My first aid training kicks in; I quickly rush to her side, dropping to my knees. Yuriko is clearly having an epileptic seizure, so I yank my jacket off, roll it up and place her head on it, maintaining it in place and speaking soothingly to her. Björn snaps out of it and ask me what to do, so I warn him against restraining her movements and ask him instead to push all the furniture away, so the woman doesn't bang herself any further. They follow my instructions and I check my watch. Little by little Yuriko calms down and I place her in the recovery position.

'The last seizure was more than five minutes long,' I tell Aileen. 'She needs an ambulance.'

'I've already called 999,' she says.

DeAnn returns to the room and seeing the situation, checks what I've done and says, 'I'm a doctor, I'll take it from here.'

Stroking Yuriko's forehead, I push her long hair out of the way as DeAnn takes her pulse.

Who would have known that all those years of volunteering as a fire marshal on my floor would pay off? Well, if nothing else comes out of today, at least I'll have helped this poor woman.

The other candidates have formed little groups standing away from us and are all chatting loudly now. As the young woman comes to, I whisper soothingly to her but she hides her face in her hands and starts to cry.

The paramedics finally arrive and take Yuriko away. As they go, I grab her notebook and pen and tuck them under her, placing her hand on them. She looks at me gratefully, too tired to speak, as the EMTs wheel her out of the room.

'Ahem.' Theodora McArthur pats her bun. Andrew and Critchlow are standing next to her. Aileen returns, closing the door behind her and comes to stand next to them.

Theodora McArthur continues, 'We are now ready to announce the names of the eight candidates who'll be moving on to the next round. Everyone, please have a seat.'

She looks around the room sternly and everyone sobers up and starts righting chairs and rearranging the furniture into a semblance of order. Once silence falls and she has everyone's attention, Professor McArthur pulls out a small, white piece of paper from her jacket pocket and unfolds it, watching us above her glasses.

'DeAnn.' The American barely looks surprised.

'Björn.' He straightens up and thrusts out his large chest.

'Frank.' The pinstriped cockney guy smirks and raises his head, looking around at the losers.

'Andika.' The intense woman squares her jaw and throws a glance at Aileen.

'Woody.' He lets out a surprised little laugh.

'Karim.' The thin man pushes his glasses up his nose and allows himself a smile, which disappears quickly.

'Adam.' A military-looking man says thank you and I recognise an Australian accent.

Oh no – I'm not selected. I've been so absorbed in the epilepsy incident that I forgot to worry over the results. Professor McArthur hesitates, frowns at her piece of paper, exchanges a glance with Andrew and says, 'Olivia.'

Relief floods over me.

Theodora McArthur folds the list and removes her glasses. 'The candidates who have not been selected, please follow Miss Foley, who will return your belongings and walk you out. Thank you all for participating.'

They file out of the room, glancing resentfully at us, and I feel blood rushing to my cheeks. How awful for them. Marjorie tries to make eye contact with Frank but he's speaking with Woody and ignores her. The freckled woman grabs the tall engineer by the arm as they exit; he seems slightly dazed and unaware that she's talking to him.

The door closes and Theodora turns her stern gaze to us. 'Congratulations, you shall now proceed to the fourth round.'

Andrew takes over. 'This is what we're able to tell you at this stage: you're competing for junior positions within the Cassandra Programme; we're looking to fill two field positions and possibly a few back-office positions, depending on your profiles.'

Karim asks, 'What does the Programme do?' He's very thin and tanned, with a mop of black hair.

'We can't tell you everything but we can start to give you the basics. We conduct year-long, data-gathering missions in foreign locations. You'll be working undercover and won't be able to disclose your true mission to anyone other than the Programme.'

'Did you just say year-long?' I ask, aghast.

'Yes, that's correct. The field missions are one year long. You also have to be prepared and trained beforehand and debriefed afterwards, so the minimum assignment length is approximately one and a half years. You need to let us know immediately if that will be an issue. If you have a family that depends on you, it will be impossible for you to make contact for a year. Similarly, if you need to take medications regularly, we would not be able to provide you with those during the year abroad, so you need to let us know and will be disqualified from the process.'

Expressions of surprise and concern dawn on the other candidates' faces.

I can't do this. What if my next IVF works? It's impossible. But if I'm honest, I'm also intrigued and the anxiety is tinged with a shimmer of excitement.

'Are the assignments dangerous?' Adam asks, his Australian accent quite pronounced.

Theodora turns her gaze on him and takes in his soldier's build. 'Yes, they can be. There have been instances where agents have died.'

That takes a minute to sink in. We look at each other. Wow, proper James Bond stuff then. Why anyone would think me qualified for ... this is absurd.

'What will the next round's format be?' Woody asks, adjusting the noose of his shiny tie, looking uncomfortable.

'It will be a two-day, off-site selection round. At the end of which, you'll be evaluated and we'll extend an offer to the two candidates whom we think are most qualified,' Andrew answers.

'Any other questions?' Theodora looks around. 'Would anybody like to drop out at this stage?'

Silence.

'Quite. In that case, I'll see you all at the next round.'

6

DEANN

H*eathrow, United Kingdom, July 2016*

THE STEWARDESS IS WAVING her arms about uselessly, trying to get someone to look at her and listen to the emergency instructions. Obviously no one does.

I'm in business class, trying to make myself comfortable as the plane taxies on the Heathrow runway. Time to leave this harebrained Programme behind and return to real life.

A kid is staring fixedly at me through the space between the seats. The toddler tried to play with me earlier and I completely ignored it, so it started throwing M&Ms at me and I had a stern conversation with the mother. Now she's offended. People get irrational about their kids. Seriously, it's not acceptable to let your kid behave that way. I bet the little creep is going to scream his lungs out during the whole flight.

I ask the flight attendant to move me when she finishes

her pointless arm milling and she frowns, puzzled, then comes back a few minutes later and confirms that she can't move me to a child-free zone. She also offers a complimentary glass of champagne to the offended mother, coos over the little monster and gives it crayons and a toy. It's going to be a long flight.

My phone beeps and the stewardess stares pointedly at the device in my hand, then leaves to scold other passengers.

'I want to fuck you tonight.' Philip's texts are not so subtle anymore.

I ponder what to type back. This is the first time he's contacted me for weeks.

My phone rings and I pick up, feeling a tremor of desire.

'Hello DeAnn.' My mother doesn't really do terms of endearment. Or small talk. 'Your father had a stroke. We spent the night in hospital.'

'Is he OK?'

'He should survive.'

'Why didn't you call me?'

'There was no point, you couldn't have done anything.'

But I'd have liked to know, I want to yell.

'When can you get here?'

I mentally run through flight schedules and the time zones. 'I can be there tomorrow evening. Send me the names of his doctors.'

'Alright, see you then.' She hangs up.

I quickly book a connecting flight from Baltimore to Miami, ignoring the flight attendant's increasingly shrill injunctions to turn my phone off, then spend the flight worrying about my father and feeling powerless to do anything about it.

· · ·

THE PLANE'S just landed in Miami and the plane's AC is already straining to compensate for the tropical humidity creeping up the aisle toward me.

I get off the plane, wheel my suitcase into the cloying heat and wait by the curb for my mom to drive up. And here she is, parking her old sedan. She doesn't get out to hug me. I didn't expect her to. I get in, clenching my teeth.

My mother's so light-skinned that she'd pass the brown paper bag test. Nowadays, most people just mistake her for a Latina. She used to be a PA, my father's PA, to be exact. He was powerful, she was young and pretty. My dad's eighty-five now, but the other wife and kids still hate us.

'You look tired. You should take better care of your skin, your wrinkles are starting to show,' she says.

We drive in silence for the most part. From time to time she asks a question about my job. My condo. Whether I've continued with the diet.

The empty streets of the quiet Miami Beach neighborhood unfurl outside my window. I look at the palm trees without seeing them, eager to escape the oppressive car. She parks and I get out, taking a deep breath of humid twilight air. Tropical plants have latched onto the blue house, suffocating it in their unruly embrace. My mother opens the front door and we're engulfed in an arctic cold as darkness surrounds us. My eyes take a minute to adjust. As I remove my shoes and sunglasses, she goes to the kitchen and pours us two glasses of icy water. She hands me one silently.

In the guestroom, I sit on the hard bed and the layer of yellow foam exhales with a moldy sigh. My hand idly runs over the moss green bedspread as I stare at the white walls, seeing without seeing the lack of paintings, childhood photos or trinkets. I unpack my bags and check my work emails. Nothing burning.

There's a knock on my door.

'Dinner.' My mother never uses three words when one will do.

We eat in silence, ham sandwiches, crusts removed, a few chips. My five-year-old self comes flooding back, curiously vivid every time I'm with her. As if being with my mom stripped me of accomplishments, erased years of therapy and carved me to the core until only the insecure child remains, toying with the flavorless food on her plate.

As soon as her plate is emptied, she excuses herself and goes to her room, closing the door behind her. I stay for a while, watch some reality TV on mute, answer my work emails, paying attention to neither. My heart is tethered to my father, sleeping alone in the hospital.

All the lights are off and my mother's door is still closed when I sneak back into my room. Despite the jetlag, I fall asleep clutching my Blackberry.

THE NIGHT IS FRAUGHT with nightmares. I gasp and wake up with a start, drenched in sweat.

My mom's already up, her hair and makeup done, when I emerge, my pajama crumpled and sweaty, hair plastered to my forehead, the pillows' creases imprinted on my left cheek. She looks at her watch and takes a sip of coffee.

She always makes me feel inadequate. Without words. Too big, too tall, too messy, not as I should be. I shower, get dressed and attempt to regain my usual self-confidence with moderate success.

We drive to the hospital.

'So how are things with Trevor?'

I'm so surprised that I don't know what to answer. I go for short and to the point. 'It's over.'

'You're not getting any younger and your looks won't last forever, you know.'

I press my lips together. 'He wasn't the right person for me.'

'So you're not intending to give me grandchildren?'

'Erm. No.'

'You'll break your father's heart. It will kill him.'

Anger rises on the left side of my skull, like mustard inadvertently swallowed. 'I didn't realize you felt so strongly about this.'

I expect her to answer but she clams up again. The journey continues in silence as I mull over how guilty I feel now. How strange. I was always quite sure about not wanting any children and I didn't feel the need to justify it, but somehow she's once again made me feel like an underachiever who's selfishly causing pain to her loved ones.

How does she do that? We must have exchanged a total of twenty words. I need to cut this stay short. I don't know how much more of this I can take. It's going to cost me a fortune in therapy.

Finally we get to the hospital. It's just as well because we've both run out of topics. Busy puke-colored corridors and beeping sounds greet us. The smell of urine and sweat mixes with disinfectant. She leads me through the busy hallways to a wide room where six pitiful forms lie on hospital beds emitting groans of pain. Dad is in the farthest bed, by the window, looking frail. My heart clenches at the sight of his pitiful smile.

I hurry over to him and grab his hand; it feels thin and bony, the skin like parchment. I stroke it, careful to avoid the cannula but the syringe digs into his flesh every time he moves his hand.

His eyes are milky around the edges and his face is lined. My heart contracts in my chest. He was once a giant.

My father coming home from work, wearing a suit with pointy lapels; my mom, her seventies hair perfect, in her tunic dress and pants, rushing to greet him at the door; a kiss, his hand wrapping around her waist. Me, in orange velvet overalls, cross-legged on the floor, watching *Wonder Woman* about three inches from the screen. I watch them embrace; curious, uncomfortable, impatient. I pretend I haven't seen the kiss until my father calls, 'Little Bucket, where's my hug?' then I spring up and run toward him, jumping into his arms as he whisks me up in the air. I burst into a cascade of giggles, conscious of my mother's gaze. My little legs wriggle free of his embrace. Delighted. Dizzy. Out of breath.

Now I sit on the chair by his hospital bed and hold his brittle hand in both of mine.

'Dad?' My voice sounds smaller than usual.

'Little Bucket,' he rasps, trying to smile.

My heart twinges again. Damn it, keep it together DeAnn.

'Dad, how are you feeling?'

If I focus on the medical aspects, I should be able to manage my emotions. But my father is having none of that.

'You came.' He raises his hand slowly and strokes my cheek.

A tear rolls down my face. He wipes it away, then his arm drops on the bed, exhausted.

'I'm not leaving you yet, Little Bucket.'

'Oh good.' A smile wobbles on my lips.

My mother clears her throat and I straighten up.

'The doctor said he'll answer our questions at ten a.m.,' she says. 'We should go to his office.'

'Yes, of course.' I squeeze my father's hand, wink at him and leave the room.

'You can't cry in front of him,' my mother says dryly, as we walk down the khaki corridor together.

'I won't anymore.'

She nods, eyes straight ahead.

The doctor looks like a twelve-year-old but he answers my questions adequately enough. He indicates that the operation went well and explains the recovery plan.

An old woman stares over at us, envious, perhaps, of my father's lucky escape, as the nurse removes his IV drip, leaving his bony hand bruised and bleeding. The nurse puts a Band-Aid on it and I step out while my mother helps him dress.

We drive back, my parents in the front, Dad gazing out, absentmindedly rubbing his palm, my mother staring at the road. I'm in the back, feeling like a child again.

When we get home, we struggle to support him, unfamiliar with our new roles as his human crutches. Then we swiftly find our places in this new dance; Dad in the middle of his two girls, heaving, stumbling. Mom leads, opening doors, I follow, relishing the feel of his arm around my shoulders, carrying the bag of medications and closing doors.

We half carry, half walk him to the bed and I get a glimpse of his thin legs, his protruding ribs, the bruises as he slips under the covers. I swallow to release the painful ball that has formed in my throat.

'There you go. All done, Dad.'

'Bessie dear, could you make me a coffee, please?' My

mother nods and leaves. A few moments later, muted clattering noises trickle in from the kitchen.

My father is lying propped up on a few pillows; he pats the bed next to him.

'What's wrong, Little Bucket?'

'Nothing.' I shrug.

My father sees right through my cheerful façade.

'Your mom doesn't know how to cope with this situation. But you do. You've always been strong.'

I nod.

He hesitates. 'Your mother told me about Trevor. You shouldn't marry the wrong man just to please us.' He struggles with his breath and has to stop.

'You don't mind about me not wanting children?'

'I just want you to be happy. Don't worry about us old folks. Go live your life. Enjoy it to the fullest. Look at me.' He gestures to his spent body. 'I was twenty years old just yesterday.' He laughs softly and it sounds like coughing.

I smile, feeling slightly better.

'I named you, you know,' he says, a faraway look in his eyes.

Actually, I didn't know.

'I named you for the Greek goddess of the hunt. I wanted you to be fierce and strong. You were never meant for an ordinary life, DeAnn. But I worry sometimes... I worry about you, Little Bucket.'

'Oh, Dad, please don't worry, I'm fine—'

He waves my protests away. 'You know, when the Man up there lets me into Heaven, He won't ask me if I've worked enough or earned enough money. He'll ask me if I've loved enough.' My father takes a wheezing breath and continues, 'I know that love hurts and that it rocks the boat. I know that sometimes it can be hard to let someone in. But sometimes, Little Bucket, when you let your door unlock, when you open up, sometimes, joy will come in – and life and meaning.'

Jarred, I nod and kiss him on the cheek. It feels stubbly and wrinkled.

'You have to find a way to open up and connect to others, Little Bucket, otherwise, think of all they'll miss.' He smiles.

My father always does that. Impart wisdom at the most unexpected times. I love him as I've never loved anyone else in my life. He pats my hand and falls asleep as old people do, mid-blink.

I sit very still on the bed, holding his wounded hand, stroking it, as my mind tugs, taking me back to the strange interviews. On the one hand, it would be completely unreasonable to take a position with the Cassandra Programme. Everything I have done since I graduated has been designed to achieve comfort and safety. It took me long enough to reimburse my student loans and amass a nest egg, I'm loath to blow it all on a ridiculous career move to this mystery organization. How would I even justify that in my resume? It's preposterous.

On the other hand, I'm really tempted. This seems to resonate with my father's advice. What if I could take a dramatically different road and somehow stumble on my joy? The Programme sounds more exciting than my current job and it could be just the jolt I need to snap me out of my empty, emotionless life. I have been worried lately that maybe I don't feel enough and am struggling to know what to do about it. Well, maybe this is just the ticket.

The door opens. The aroma of coffee spreads in the room as my mother deposits a small tray on the nightstand and closes the door behind her.

The rest of the day passes in a daze. I have a thorough

look at the drugs and explain everything to my mother, prepare a pill dispenser and leave all the phone numbers prominently displayed for her.

As the day draws to a close, I kiss Dad goodbye and he squeezes my forearm, tapping it gently with unspoken words of affection.

WE'RE NEARING the airport when my mother finally speaks up, breaking the silence of the ride.

'You stole him away from me.'

I must have misheard her. She looks at the road intently.

'From the moment you were born, I ceased to exist for him. You stole all his attention and love away from me.'

I have no idea what to say to her, so I stay quiet.

'You were the sun to him. From the day you appeared, his life started to revolve around you. He likes me. But he loves you.'

'Mom, I don't think—'

She cuts across me, 'Just be worthy of it, DeAnn.'

I close my mouth and look at her profile.

Can she really believe what she's saying? I understand now why she was so sad throughout my life, why she never really warmed to me. But even if it's true, what could I possibly have done about it? I could hardly avoid being born.

We reach the airport and I get out of the car. She stays seated, as usual. I pick up my suitcase and walk to her window. Our eyes meet through the glass, then she drives off, leaving me alone on the sidewalk. Slightly abandoned.

Then I snap out of it. She can't abandon me. I'm a self-sufficient 42-year-old woman. I'm a renowned geneticist, I own a bay-view condo and I have a life to go back to.

I shake myself awake and walk toward the terminal, catching floating strands of my character as I go, weaving them back into my tapestry, thread by thread. Strength, conviction, determination, intelligence: catch, weave. Catch again.

When I land in Baltimore, the tapestry is nearly whole again. A gap here and there betraying the strain of the week-end, but definitely, recognizably me.

It's time for a change in my life.

7

OLIVIA

L*ondon, United Kingdom, August 2016*

Bruises are blossoming on either side of my belly button like strange butterflies, their dark purplish wings moving slowly under my skin. There, in the soft, plush sanctuary of my womb, my child is hesitating, wondering if this will be the right place for his soul to come into the world.

I trace the contours of the injection stains and imagine little Max assessing us, deciding what kind of parents we will be, as his infinitely small shape hovers. Maybe he will latch on if I remain very still and send him all the love I can muster.

'I can't do this.'

Rain is pouring outside. Martin is at the foot of our bed, looking out of the window, fully dressed.

'Sorry – what?' I say.

'I can't bear the weather, Mousey. I'm moving back to Malta.'

Being in London is obviously making Martin miserable. I'm asking too much of him. I love him so much.

'It's just for six months,' he pleads, his eyes welling up.

My heart clenches with compassion. He's trying his best. I should find it in my heart to let him go, if he needs it so badly.

'OK, Bear, if it's so important for you. But why?'

'I need to go because you're pregnant. So you're going to start puking and you're going to get fat and I don't want to be here for that. Also, it's summer in Malta and I want to be at the beach.'

I spend another two weeks trying to convince him to stay.

The Two-Week Wait.

Every twitch, every cramp, every spot at the bottom of my knickers is perhaps the embryo implanting.

Every craving, every hot flash, every swelling is the pregnancy starting.

Every thought, every hope, every action is aimed, taut and quivering at my dream; Max's blond curls shining in the sun, Max's laughter pealing like a wind chime's tinkle, Max's hand in mine, small warm and perfect.

THEN THE DAY COMES.

Negative.

Hands shaking, I fight to open the second pregnancy test, my sweaty palms slick on the plastic packaging.

Negative again.

I take the test six times and decide it doesn't mean anything.

Until finally, my period comes.

Cramps, like the muffled grumblings of a storm, wake me up in the night. Then pain's hot poker jabs at my insides and, finally, the reality cannot be denied, as I get up in the dark, blindly groping towards the bathroom.

Blood flows.

Dark red and velvety.

I fall on the cold tiled floor, hugging my knees, and crumple into the most compact ball of misery I can manage. I sit there, no tears left in me. Just emptiness.

Game over.

Martin leaves for Malta a few days later. Two days in, he texts: it's over.

And so, sometimes God says no.

No to your most fervent prayers, your hopes, your dreams.

I'm left in London, on my own, inhaling chocolate, cakes and sweets like there's no tomorrow. Because there is no tomorrow.

My life has imploded.

I've just spent the last four years on a diet, drinking no alcohol, saving, planning my entire life around the IVF cycles. I've gradually cut off all my single friends who partied too hard or who simply didn't have kids, because I thought of myself already as a mother. I got closer to the ones who did have kids but I never belonged in that circle either. I've slowed down my career on purpose in order to have a manageable schedule for when the baby came. But he never did.

This was the only goal I could not attain by sheer force

of will, hard work or smarts. The one goal that depended on my body and God. Neither one saw fit to grant my wish.

Now I find myself with a mediocre career, no man, no child, significantly less money, old and fat from all the hormone injections.

Time to eat Nutella with a spoon. Time to binge on TV series and whinge to my friends about an outcome they all saw coming two months into this relationship.

Wasn't I meant for bigger, better things? I feel like an actress who received the wrong part. This isn't my life. Heck, this isn't even the right movie.

I can see all the decisions along the way that led me to this point and yet it makes no sense that I am here. I have no idea what to do next. What am I for? Who am I for? I make no difference in anyone's life and if I died right now, I'd barely leave a ripple behind me, on the surface of my friends' lives. I'm clinging on to a borrowed desk, pretending that my job serves a purpose, but helping a law firm to get richer has got to be one of the most pointless ways to spend a life.

Maybe I should simply continue with the mysterious job interviews. I haven't got anything left to lose, to be honest. I couldn't possibly be successful in the Cassandra Programme, though. The usual berating starts in my head without me even noticing: 'I'm a middle-aged spinster who's overweight and out of shape; the last thing they need is me on some field assignment. I failed at everything, I can't even manage to find a boyf...' The familiar record skids to a halt.

I barely have one or two years left to meet another man, go through the whole rigmarole of dating again and then get to the point where we can try for a baby. Oh God, oh God, oh God, what if I've missed the boat? What if I remain childless forever?

The singsong voice chants inside my head, as it usually does, except today it doesn't sing about everything turning out OK. Today, it starts singing in a loop: '*I want to die, I want to die, I want to die, I want to die, I want to die, I want to die.*' On and on from the moment I open my eyes in the morning until my head hits the pillow at night and I surrender to merciful oblivion.

8

DEANN

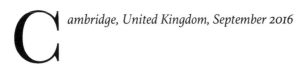

ambridge, United Kingdom, September 2016

'Ahem.'

The college porter is wearing a black suit and a bowler hat. A bowler hat, for Christ's sake. He looks at me with all the disdain usually reserved for tourists and cockroaches.

'I'm here for an interview.'

'Name?'

'DeAnn Carpenter.'

He disappears inside his lodge and reappears a minute later at the window, looking at a large, leather-bound ledger.

'Yes...' He pauses. 'You appear to be on my list.' He sounds surprised.

I snatch the visitor's badge and keys from his hand before he changes his mind, and drag my suitcase through a long corridor, then up a stone spiral staircase to a small spartan room on the first floor. A desolate twin bed of the industrial metal-tube variety is huddled against a wall smallpoxed with Blu Tack. The rest of the furniture consists of a rickety nightstand and a scuffed desk/chair combo, and yet the room feels crowded, as it's 150 square feet at most.

'You've got to be kidding me.' Sighing and cursing under my breath, I unpack and change into tight black jeans and a bright green silk blouse. I know better than to mistake tonight's dinner for casual networking; this is part of the selection process, of course. I put on my large emerald ring and my green Louboutin pumps and look at myself in the spotted mirror above the sink. Everything is in place; my modern battle gear. You need to be perfect to show strength. People don't respect the weak, so I make a point of always appearing collected, polished, immaculate. The skin-tight jeans hug my thighs nicely. I've worked hard to tone them, so I'm pleased to see the results looking good.

As I step into the hallway, Woody comes out of his room, a few doors down. He sees me and saunters over, trying to ingratiate himself to me with a few oily compliments but I can't lose sight of the fact that we're competing, so I give him a polite smile and keep quiet. His keen face is turned up toward me as I'm taller than him to begin with and the heels aren't helping.

We get to the reception room and even I have to admit that it looks impressive; antique wood paneling covers the walls and the ceiling's exposed beams curve inward like the inside of a ship. Tall mullioned windows let in the fading light of the sunset, while logs burn in a stone fireplace.

A few tables are laid with white cloths and elaborate place settings. Woody is still prattling on and I let him follow me as I locate a waiter and order a glass of Rioja.

Most of the others have arrived and are mingling with the Programme recruiters. Andrew Catterwall is already talking to Olivia, sitting on a sofa by the fire. Her unruly red curls stand out against her pale freckled skin. She's sitting with her feet turned inward, hunched over with her arms crossed, as if protecting her middle.

I think idly about how stunning she'd look if she straightened up, wore heels and crossed her legs. A good tailored dress would do wonders to showcase her hourglass figure, but her clothes are baggy and gray, she's not wearing enough makeup and a little silver cross hangs around her neck. One of those do-gooders who can't wait to pop out six kids, then. I bet she's overemotional and always gets dumped because she's too obvious about wanting to get married. I can't stand her type. Her chirpy friendliness grates. Maybe she does it on purpose, to look harmless, and the worst part is that it seems to be working; Andrew laughs at something she's just said.

Canapés start circulating and I join the group by the intricately carved fireplace, careful to sit as far as possible from that douchebag, Frank. He's looking pleased with himself, speaking loudly to Aileen in his irritating cockney accent. I'm pretty sure he banged the bimbo back in London. Stupid girl, you should never mix business and pleasure and she got played. Frank, I bet, knew exactly what he was doing.

Dinner starts and I find myself seated between Adam and Karim, listening distractedly to their conversation as I really couldn't care less about sports. I use the time to look around and assess the other contestants.

Woody spends his evening trying to brown-nose everyone from the Programme and mostly ignores the other candidates. Probably a technique that worked for him at the UN, but I'm not so sure it will be very effective here.

Whatever else the Programme is, it's a professional team and a well-oiled machine. I get the distinct impression that every move we make is under scrutiny. The food is better than I'd have expected from a British kitchen and the conversation flows easily among the contestants.

Slightly red in the face, Frank becomes much too loud and his hands start to wander. Aileen looks increasingly alarmed, her bony arms making small jerking motions as she tries to evade the unwanted groping. Theodora and Andrew exchange glances, he gets up and smoothly asks Aileen to get him something from the office, leaving Frank thwarted but none the wiser about his *faux pas*.

Across from me, Björn is talking in low whispers with Critchlow, as Andika quietly listens in. These two are the most capable looking. They don't wear fatigues or uniforms but their demeanor gives them away. I wonder about the diverse range of candidates. What sort of person are they looking for? How can we all qualify if we're so different?

Apparently, we'll go through a day of interviews tomorrow and a day of physical testing on Sunday so I imagine we'll find out soon enough who they're looking for.

THE FIRST MORNING is broken up into short exercises and passes quickly. They're testing us individually to learn whether we're able to find threads between seemingly disparate groups of information. Analytical reasoning, logic, deduction. Once I spot that this is what they are looking for, each test becomes easier. We take the Myers Briggs person-

ality test (INTJ, no surprise there), IQ tests, logic tests – and I
fly easily through it all.

In the afternoon, we're tested as teams. They put us
through thirty-minute simulations and pair us up to evaluate who works best with whom. The exercises range from
responding to an armed kidnapping to working together to
convince another team to do something for us.

My strong personality and independence don't sit well
with the men. The pairing with Frank is probably the one
that goes worst. We're instructed to build a wooden catapult
with Ikea-type instructions, but we both try to take control
and end up arguing about how to do it and run out of time.
He's so disappointed to fail that he starts throwing insults
and racial slurs at me. I manage to keep my anger in check
only because Olivia comes by, and, under cover of helping
me pick up the various pieces to put them away, whispers
'two-way mirror' in my ear. Startled and puzzled as to why
she would help me, I nod and leave Frank to his rant,
walking calmly away from him.

Surprisingly my fire alarm test with the Good Samaritan
goes really well as she easily submits to my leadership but
makes sensible suggestions. Olivia follows my instructions
without quibbling, so we arrive first.

At the end of the day, we're given a fifty-page brief and
two hours to prepare a presentation. We must all do it
together. My idea of hell on earth. They all sit around a large
conference table, arguing while Björn, Olivia and I behave
sensibly. It seems we're the only ones to know that we're
being observed. The others think we're alone and that the
presentation is the actual point. It isn't, of course. I'm
starting to feel like a lab rat.

Olivia very subtly ends up convincing everyone to go her
way. She does it almost unconsciously, just by asking kindly

and using the connection she's established with each person. God, she's irritating.

I sit apart from everyone, on a leather sofa, as they come up with the presentation's content, and I let them muddle through for a while. Eyes semi-closed, I observe the group's dynamics. When they've all exhausted themselves arguing over nothing, I swoop in and shed light on a couple of the key points they've overlooked. They all look at me, surprised; I guess they thought I was sleeping.

From that point on, the group starts arguing about who will present, all keen to look good and to take credit. I suspect none of it matters, though. Miss Goody Two-shoes ends up getting everyone to agree reluctantly to equal speaking time.

When the time is up and the interviewers come back in the room, we take turns presenting our group's conclusions. Björn is too succinct and leaves out crucial nuances. Woody is too verbose and goes off on a particularly cringe-worthy improvised tangent at one point. Frank makes a few inappropriate jokes, the kind that no doubt usually get raucous laughter from his trader colleagues, but they fall flat here.

Andika gives a military-style debrief. Adam delivers an efficient but uninspiring presentation. Karim gets lost in the fine points of theory, his thin arms flailing about as he gets more and more stressed.

So Olivia and I stand out, explaining things well, adding relevant information where necessary and stopping short of giving too many details. Her legal background probably means she's accustomed to giving talks to senior management and I, of course, am very comfortable as well, having to interact with the board of my hospital on a regular basis.

As, we're given a free evening. I excuse myself and return to my room's blissful silence and spend the rest of the evening reading the biography of the molecular biologist Francis Crick, which, appropriately enough, is set in the mediocrity of middle-class England.

With a start, at 10 p.m., I remember that I haven't checked my work emails all day. I decide to have a look at them really quickly to deal with any emergencies and end up working until 1 a.m.

9

OLIVIA

*C*ambridge, United Kingdom, September 2016

LAST NIGHT WAS LOVELY. Most of the candidates ended up in a pub down the road and as I wake up in the snug little room, I smile, remembering Woody's funny antics and Adam's botched karaoke attempt. His song is stuck in my head and I hum it as I get ready. I feel inexplicably happy. I guess I'm always on the chirpy side, but this experience is giving me hope. Hope that my life may change, that I could become something I've never imagined I could be.

The competition is tough and today might wither my happy mood; we're starting the dreaded physical tests. I'm not exactly what you might call fit and given how extremely able the other candidates are, I wouldn't be surprised to be disqualified at the end of the day.

I put on the black leggings and baggy t-shirt that I bought at Primark in a rush, as I don't own any sports gear. I tie my brand-new trainers, tighten my ponytail and hurry down the hallway towards the kitchen. Or that's where I think I'm going. But soon enough, I'm lost in the maze of corridors of the unfamiliar college.

I have no sense of direction whatsoever. I can go somewhere ten times and still get hopelessly lost on the eleventh time. Martin thought at first that I was pretending in order to make him feel manly. But a few weeks into the relationship he sounded amazed when he said, 'You really have absolutely no idea where you are, Mousey?' and I really, really didn't.

There's no point in thinking about Martin now, I chide myself. He's gone for good Olivia, think of something else.

I'm not exactly late yet, so I take the opportunity to explore the college while trying not to panic. A little shudder of excitement and stress squirms in my gut as I trespass into places I'm pretty sure I'm not supposed to see.

I hesitate and choose a hallway, walking slowly along in the eerie silence until it opens up into an atrium flooded with light. In front of me, there is a large marble plaque carved with names. Two paintings are positioned on either side of it and I approach the painting on the right, frowning.

My breath catches. It can't be – my father is looking back at me from the gilded frame. It's him. It's definitely his smile, his chin jutting out, his white hair. I bend to look at his name, written on a small golden plaque. Yes, 'Alastair Sagewright (1938–2001)'.

A hand grabs my shoulder, making me flinch.

'Oh, Andrew!' I sound shrill, I think. 'What? How—?' I don't even know what to ask, as my eyes boomerang back to the painting.

Andrew looks at me kindly and gestures to a bench by the opposite wall. 'Take a seat, Olivia.'

I drop on the bench, eyes still glued to my dad, who is gazing down fondly at me, his hands crossed over his knee, his little knowing smile exactly as I remember it. I wrench myself away and turn to Andrew, who's observing me.

'We didn't know when to tell you this, but now is as good a time as any, I suppose.'

'Tell me what?'

'Your father went missing in the line of duty, while he was leading a mission for the Cassandra Programme. Nobody knows what happened to him.'

'But that can't be.' My mind is struggling to make sense of this. 'He was a businessman. He died in the twin towers, he was visiting one of his businesses and... and...' I stammer, starting to piece things together, my mind spinning.

They never recovered his body. He was gone for a whole year, supposedly attending to his business venture. Mum thought he'd left her.

We had no idea he was in New York. It was only several weeks after 9/11 that we received word he had died in the terrible event. Apparently the forensic investigators had worked out that he was there and it took a long time for them to confirm his DNA and send us word. Mum and I had watched the news horrified, like everyone else, not realising that he had died along with the thousands of other poor souls. We had a funeral with an empty coffin.

I'd always hoped in the back of my mind that it had all been a horrible mistake, that he was never in the towers and that he'd appear on our doorstep, fifteen years later, with a big smile on his face.

A lump forms in my throat. Even with so little knowledge about the Programme, I can already tell that the circumstances match.

'I'm so sorry, Olivia.'

Andrew puts a tentative hand on my shoulder. I let the tears roll down my cheeks, making splats of wet on the bench's green leather. He gives me a proper handkerchief to wipe my eyes and we wait in silence for my sorrow genie to creep back into its dusty bottle.

At length, Andrew gets up and offers me his hand. We walk over to the marble plaque on the wall and I run my hand along the letters of my father's name. There are dozens of others in neat rows below his. Nora Haq, Max Breville, Tim Fairmont, Rohan Shah. They mean nothing to me. Other agents, I guess. What did they die for?

'What was so important? What was he doing?'

'Unfortunately I can't tell you that. Yet.'

'I need to pass first?'

'Yes.'

To the right of the list of names, virgin marble looms, shot through with dark veins. Enough space for another three rows at least. So they're expecting more deaths. I shiver and take a last look at my dad's kind face.

'We'd better get back before today's round starts,' Andrew says, gently guiding me as we walk back to the kitchen together.

'Sorry I got lost. I've the worst sense of direction,' I say, absentmindedly.

'We know,' Andrew answers with a smile. 'We've been following you, learning about you. We think you may have the potential to make it here.'

'I don't stand a chance against all the alpha males strutting around this bloody place.'

'Give yourself some credit, Olivia, most of the candidates failed the previous round. They weren't as smart, as observant or as empathetic as you.'

'I'm sure you meant pathetic,' I sniffle.

He laughs and pats my back. 'See, you're making jokes. Feeling better already, then?'

'Thank you, Andrew.'

'You know,' he says, a faraway look in his eyes, 'we used to send exclusively non-military personnel on missions. We still do sometimes. You'd make a really good field agent.'

It's hard not to snort. I remember Dad ignoring me and looking bored when I tried to connect with him. He clearly thought I wasn't interesting enough, not smart enough to share anything with. What am I trying to accomplish? It's too late to gain his approval – and I might die in the process, trying to fit in his world.

We walk the rest of the way in silence.

The others are nearly done with their breakfasts, but I can't eat. Aileen comes over and asks if I'm OK. I nod as Frank makes a lewd joke about Andrew and me arriving together at breakfast and Woody laughs. Andika looks at me suspiciously but says nothing.

Everybody leaves except Aileen. We fall behind the rest of the group on our way to the gym and I tell her what happened in a whisper.

'I'm sorry, Olivia. My father died too.' She swallows back a painful memory and I recognise the feeling.

The gym smell like all other gyms – of dried sweat, old socks and misery. I already feel inadequate as our voices echo under the high ceiling and we're instructed to take evenly spaced positions from each other.

We start with general flexibility exercises and I'm pleased to see my fertility-boosting yoga classes pay off. Björn is struggling with the simplest poses and Frank isn't even trying but gets redder and redder anyway. Then we move on to endurance. We run ten kilometres. I arrive second to last but at least I finish, unlike Woody. They test our ability to get out of restraints, to make knots; they have us remember a sequence of steps and repeat them. I do quite well at that actually as it requires memory rather than physical skill.

I fail time and again to climb up the rope dangling in front of my nose as I stare at DeAnn's perfect behind hanging six feet up. I'm debating whether to give up and walk away when I hear Karim whisper to Andika, 'I'm not surprised. She's only made it this far because her dad once managed the Programme.'

But Andrew's words are ringing in my head: 'I can't tell you anything *yet*.' He thinks I can make it. I have to. Otherwise I'll never know what happened to my dad.

A wave of determination washes over me and, ignoring them, I concentrate on the rope-climbing technique and try it again and again until my palms are bleeding, until the insides of my blobby thighs are one giant purple bruise – until I finally touch the ceiling.

Then they test our self-defence skills. Adam and DeAnn give us an extremely impressive demonstration of Krav Maga. I didn't even know what it was until today and would have guessed that it was a seventies crochet pattern. Turns out it's the scariest self-defence method there is.

Asked to try a few self-defence poses with Björn, I spend the next hour being slammed to the floor, as he showcases his brute strength instead of actually teaching me the methods. But each time he throws me to the mat, I get back up and try again. The others are better equipped than me: fit, strong, trained; they already know what to do. I'll have to learn. But I can at least show the examiners that I won't give up.

At last, the day ends with a comprehensive series of psychological tests and finally an interview with a psychiatrist. I have to wait in line for my turn, as one by one the candidates come out, looking destabilised, relieved or exhausted. Frank and I are the last ones left when he turns to me with a sneer on his face. I groan mentally – what now?

'So, your daddy used to work here,' he whispers.

'How did you...?'

'You're grossly underqualified for this job.' His stale breath hits my face as he leans in. I try to turn away but he's too close. 'Quit now and let someone with a real chance take over. You're a waste of space – look at yourself, you're ridiculous.' I feel my self-confidence crumbling as his glance travels down my sweaty t-shirt and sausagey legs encased in the too-tight spandex.

'Olivia?' An older woman with lacquered blonde hair peers at her clipboard and then at me.

I quickly slip into the psychiatrist's office and slump on the armchair, breathing in. This is easier than jogging and facing off bullies, so I relax and talk to her candidly. If she's evaluating our psychological ability to cope with the job, there's no point in lying, so I go with the truth. It goes well, as far as I can tell.

As the day draws to an end, we're all summoned to the main hall again. Today there are no dressed tables and no evening wear. We're all in tracksuits and the jury is lined up behind a long table, waiting for us. The other candidates are already standing in the corridor outside when I arrive. They're going to announce the results.

Even though we can't hear what they're saying, the conversation doesn't seem to be going well. Professor McArthur is frowning, Critchlow looks pleased with himself and Andrew is chopping the air with his hands, intense and unhappy. Finally, they come to some sort of agreement, which doesn't seem to satisfy any of them. Aileen waves to the attendant to let us through and we instinctively form a line in front of the judges.

'Thank you all for participating in this selection process,' Professor McArthur starts. 'Most of you came from abroad and had to carve out the time in your diaries, and we really appreciate it.'

All of us stay quiet, holding our breath.

'Well, there's no point in delaying any longer. We're filling two field agent positions and we have selected Björn and Andika. Congratulations to both, your marks were excellent.'

My heart sinks. It was a long shot but I really wanted to be selected. I will never know what happened to my father now. I start to turn to the buff Swedish man to congratulate him but Theodora holds up her hand and motions for us to be quiet.

'Just a moment, I'm not quite done. This year, it was quite difficult to select the best two candidates as you all had different strengths and assets. After much deliberation, we have decided to offer Olivia and DeAnn positions as well, in the legal and medical team, respectively.'

My heart leaps. Oh my God, I'm in! DeAnn is hiding it well but I think she's pleased as well. She walks over to the table of examiners and shakes their hands, thanking each one in turn. So professional, always.

I'm thinking of doing the same when Frank comes over, pretends to shake my hand but instead grabs my wrist and crushes it in his big meaty grip, as he yanks me towards him.

'Daddy's girl has won, what a surprise,' he whispers.

Adam comes over and elbows him in the ribs, directing a sideways look at the jury.

'Let them hear me, I want them to,' Frank says more loudly.

'I agree, this process is clearly rigged.' Adam eyes me up and down and shakes his head.

Woody walks over and asks me, in a seemingly friendly way, 'So what did you do? Sleep with Andrew?'

I'm unsuccessfully trying to pull my hand free of Frank's grip when Aileen appears at my side and asks, 'Everything OK here?'

They scatter reluctantly and she follows them from the corner of her eye until they're out of the room, then gently takes my wrist and inspects it. 'You'll have bruises.'

'I'll live.' I smile.

'Us girls have to stick together, don't you think? Especially now that you're going to face life-and-death situations for a living. Welcome to the Cassandra Programme.'

She pats my shoulder and walks back to the table.

Crikey, what on earth have I gotten myself into?

10

DEANN

C ambridge, United Kingdom, September 2016

I WAS PRETTY sure I'd be selected but I didn't expect the rosary rattler to make the cut as well. After she announced the results, Professor McArthur invited Olivia, Björn, Andika and me into her office. Critchlow and Andrew Catterwall also came along.

We're all gathered in a light-filled room overlooking the campus lawn. The walls are lined with bookshelves, the books double stacked and forming piles on the desk and on the floor. The place smells of paper, lavender and leather. Andrew pulls a leather armchair closer to the desk while Critchlow stands with his back against the door-jamb, looking somehow like he's guarding it against intruders. Olivia and I sit on the chairs opposite Professor McArthur's desk and Björn removes a pile of books from an ottoman, then sits on it, slightly hunched, too large for the small footstool. Aileen joins us, carrying a tray of mugs, and circulates among us; Andika declines and simply leans against a bookshelf, watching everyone from a distance.

Finally, when everyone's settled, Theodora McArthur sits at her desk, laces her fingers together and looks up at each one of us over her large glasses. A ray of sunshine is playing with dust flecks, spilling golden light over Theodora's shoulder and onto the blue rug that covers the floorboards. In the silence, a clock is ticking the seconds and the sounds of the campus below us feel remote and absurdly boisterous.

Professor McArthur speaks in a low voice: 'Björn, Andika, Olivia, DeAnn, well done. Very few candidates ever make it this far. Some years, we do not select anyone. I cannot overstate how important it is to recruit the right candidates for this job.'

Björn throws a glance at me, eyebrows raised, but it's obvious he doesn't know either what this is all about.

'At the beginning of the 1990s, I was approached to participate in a new business venture. A young theoretical physicist thought she'd had a breakthrough and the businessman who was funding this venture needed a person he trusted to test its practical applications.'

'Our team worked on it for months but had very little to report. Nothing worked. We were getting ready to abandon our efforts and I must say that I wasn't surprised, as the theory we were testing was, shall we say... far-fetched. But after months of failed attempts, one parameter was accidentally modified and it worked.'

'What worked?' I ask, losing patience.

'We can only reveal this to field agents and a few back-office personnel after thorough vetting and clearing.'

'Will we get cleared, at our levels?' I ask, glancing at Olivia.

'Yes. It will take one month. While we vet you, you'll go through the onboarding process,' Andrew says. 'This is worth it, believe me.'

Theodora continues, 'For now, you just need to know that you'll be part of an initiative that is changing the world on an unprecedented scale. Although I cannot give you details about the Cassandra Programme yet, I can tell you that we're operating at the cutting edge of science.'

The Girl Scout next to me is biting her lower lip, frowning. Andika just watches all of us impassively, like a cat gauging mice. Professor McArthur waits for a moment and when no questions come, she continues.

'After the initial discovery, we continued to experiment and finally, in the year 2000, we conducted our first manned mission, which successfully proved that the technology was viable. That's when we went from being a scientific team to a professional organization with field operatives.'

'You're describing events that happened over fifteen years ago. Surely by now, you'd have gone public, if this were legit,' Björn says.

Critchlow frowns. 'This isn't the type of equipment that can be commercialized or even made public, Magnusson. In the wrong hands, this technology could disrupt society on an unthinkable scale.'

I'm dubious but I decide to assume for a minute that they've found something really big. A piece of technology or weaponry that would really change the global balance of power. Just to test the logic. If it's really true, then I'd probably have managed the Cassandra Programme much like they did: keeping it under wraps, only involving a handful of trustworthy governments and I would cherry-pick the candidates without telling them anything about the real objective. It makes sense.

This could be the opportunity of a lifetime.

Agent Critchlow takes off his glasses, wipes them thoroughly and puts them back on. 'We're dealing with very dangerous knowledge so this is why, after the initial mission, it quickly became apparent that we needed to increase security and bring the operations up to a more professional level.'

Professor McArthur looks distinctly unhappy with Critchlow's statement but he carries on, unperturbed: 'I was called in to recruit and supervise the armed units at that point and I continue to oversee the training of all field agents to this day.'

'Will we go on mission right away?' Andika asks, arms crossed, fingers tapping impatiently on her arm.

'No, of course not, this isn't the sort of thing you can improvise,' Critchlow answers.

I was thinking of quitting my current position anyway; of course, I wasn't expecting my next job to be this different and confidential but it sounds interesting for a change. I wonder if it's espionage. It definitely sounds like they're sending their agents somewhere. But where?

'All four of you are going to undergo basic orientation for two weeks. Then Olivia and DeAnn will start their positions in the medical and legal teams, and Björn and Andika, you'll go on to receive six more months of training before you're sent into the field.'

With just a few years of investment of my time, I could get a glimpse into science that the rest of society hasn't even begun to dream of. If they need me, it must be something genetics-related... I could exponentially further my career with that kind of knowledge. I could figure out what companies to invest in, multiply my capital and retire early. It's only a couple of years. I'm smart, I could figure out what this technology is, even if they're not prepared to tell me yet.

There are so many unanswered questions, so many risks. But I already know – I'm going to do this.

11

OLIVIA

Cambridge, United Kingdom, October 2016

WHEN I ARRIVED in Cambridge for the two weeks of orientation, I took my quarters in the same room as before. This time, a lot more people were milling around, agents and operatives going about their business, mostly ignoring me and the rest of the back-office staff. My time was spent learning about the job, meeting my new colleagues and searching for a flat to rent near the college.

Early on in the training, Theodora approached me and motioned me to follow her. 'I hear you've learned about your father's involvement in the Programme?'

I nodded.

'I wanted to tell you much earlier but was outvoted. I'm glad you know. He was a good friend.'

Did I meet her once, a long time ago? I frowned as something itched in the back of my mind but no clear memory surfaced.

'Thank you, Professor McArthur.'

'Well then, since the cat's out of the bag, follow me.'

She took me to a lower floor, somewhere in the basement, and I followed her, wondering what this was all about. Finally we arrived at a door marked 'Archives'. She opened it and turned on the light. As the fluorescent lights blinked to life, row upon row of shelves appeared, laden with cardboard boxes, ledgers and binders. The place was huge.

Theodora walked over to a glass booth, opened the door and waited for me to get in beside her, flicking a hand up to show me the cameras.

'You'll be under surveillance at all times here,' she said, as she tapped her fingers lightly a pile of cardboard folders. 'Everything is here, in case you ever want to know. You can ask me too.' She patted my shoulder and she left me there. Puzzled, I picked up one of the dusty boxes; my father's name was on every page. The binding simply said '1993' so I grabbed an armful, sat at the table, feeling the CCTV on the back of my neck, and started reading the heavily redacted sheets.

My father basically created the whole Programme. He always had access to improbable schemes and unrealistic scientists. His talent was in recognising the opportunities that could actually work. And this time was no different. He managed the Programme from its inception in 1993 until his death in 2001.

Looking back, it's no wonder he was so busy. I remember the last time I saw him. I said hurtful things. We argued in front of a young man he'd brought home for a visit. I was so upset that my father would be missing an important event I was organising for the church. I blamed him for never caring for me, never making the time to get to know me. Why was his bloody work always more important than me? I replay that conversation in my mind often. What I wouldn't give to take back those words spoken in anger. I wish we'd had more time to get to know each other. I wish, I wish...

The fact that my father was part of the Cassandra Programme opens up new ways of thinking about that weekend: who was the young man with my father? He was inconsequential before. Just a guy I'd rather hadn't witnessed the argument. But in fact he could be important. Could he have been linked to the Programme? Maybe he could tell me more about my father's death?

Now I understand that my father didn't make it to my church event because he was leaving on a mission. A one-year mission. And he couldn't tell me anything. Not why, nor where he was going.

THERE WAS SO much to take in, what with the discoveries I was making in the archives and the training courses, that during my first week of training, I started walking along the canal at lunchtime to clear my mind.

On my second walk, I noticed a shy-looking man eating a sandwich on the grass by the water. The next day, he was there again and so was I; he noticed me as well and smiled from afar.

At the beginning of the second week, he was so absorbed in his phone that he bumped into me. I apologised, he apologised, we both laughed and it naturally became a lunch date. Now we meet each other every day, sit on the grass and chat about this and that over a sandwich and a bag of crisps. Tim is a history teacher. His hair and short beard are chestnut coloured and he has kind blue eyes. He's adorably dorky, he wears corduroy shirts that he buttons all the way to the top and he speaks in a lovely sort of hesitant way. Always trying to say the right thing in the most polite way possible.

Yesterday evening, we went for a drink for the first time. The bar turned out to be more animated than we bargained for; when the lights dimmed and the loud music started, he smiled and guided me out. But not before the UV light revealed a fluorescent letter H, on the inside of his wrist, with two serpents wrapped around it. It glowed against his pale freckled skin, there one minute and gone the next. Just a nightclub stamp that disappeared when we stepped out into the busy street full of boisterous students.

Today, our usual lunch spot was taken, so we sat by a small bridge and right as we were tucking in, I freaked out when a huge spider fell off her web and into my hair. He calmly brushed it off; he was so close that I could see the freckles on his nose. He smelled of patchouli and leather. I may have imagined it but he was close to kissing me, well definitely leaning in, at any rate. But someone jogged past us and broke the moment. DeAnn. Typical. The woman's so irritating.

I get back to the Programme building smiling and the afternoon passes by in a daze. I should be concentrating on the training of course, but what if he's The One? Of course, it's way too early to be thinking about anything at all, let alone marrying him, but I can't help but daydream about what it would be like to be with Tim. Daydreams are sometimes more pleasant than reality and having no one to think about feels so... I don't know, empty I guess.

Towards the end of the day, I'm summoned to

Critchlow's office. It feels very much like the Principal is calling me for a stern talking-to. Wondering what this could be about and which physical test I failed, I sit down and wait for his latest dressing down to start. He dives right in, no pleasantries.

'How long have you been seeing this man?'

'I beg your pardon? That's none of your business.'

'Everything is my business.' He clenches his jaw.

'Gosh, that's embarrassing.' I blush. 'I've met him a couple of times for lunch by the river; we've been chatting, that's all.'

'Did you ever meet him anywhere other than a public place?'

'Oh come off it, you're not my father, Agent Critchlow.'

'Just answer the question.'

'No.'

'Don't lie to me.'

'I'm not lying. What on earth is this about?'

He stares at me intently and seems to decide I'm telling the truth. There's a look of deep distaste on his face as he continues, 'Did you notice anything about him? Anything unusual?'

'Well, he had a glow-in-the-dark stamp on his wrist yesterday. But it's nothing—'

'Describe it,' Critchlow interrupts.

'An H.' I gesture with my hands, trying to describe it. He slides a piece of paper and a pen towards me, looking serious.

'Really? Come on. It's just harmless flirting.' I shake my head and draw. When I pass it back to Critchlow, he sucks in his breath.

'Come with me.'

He marches me to Theodora's office and tells me to wait

outside as he goes in and starts a shouting match with the Professor. Standing in the corridor, staring at my shoes like a twelve-year-old who's broken a school rule, I try not to listen but can't help it. The gist of it is that he thinks I'm an insufferable goose who would be better suited to working at a hairdresser's, that he can't believe that Theodora, Aileen and Andrew outvoted him to select me and that he'd have preferred pretty much any of the other candidates. My self-esteem plummets with every bellowed invective. I can't hear what Theodora responds but she's obviously not putting up much of a fight. He finishes by telling her about Tim as proof that I'm an idiot, not even two weeks into the training and already blundering. After that, a quieter conversation takes place, which I can't hear.

At length the door swings open and a furious Critchlow bursts out of the office, not even bothering to look at me.

Theodora calls me in, asks me to close the door behind me and take a seat. Oh dear. Is she going to dismiss me? Now that I'm faced with it, I don't want to leave.

'What I'm about to tell you, Olivia, is not widely known, even amongst the Cassandra Programme personnel.' I thought she'd yell at me but instead she's calm and stern. 'You must tell no one, do you understand?'

'Erm, OK?'

'A few months after the end of your father's mission, we started noticing that documents were going missing and deduced that we'd had a breach at the facility. Shortly after that, some of our people reported being followed and we increased security. Other events and run-ins started occurring on such a scale that we soon had to face the truth: there had been a leak about the Programme.'

This explains why the documents I'm reading in the

archives are so closely guarded and redacted, and why I'm being monitored when I read them.

'That's about the time when Agent Critchlow and his men were brought in by our sponsors. To defend the Cassandra Programme from intruders and to provide an armed response unit in case of attack.'

'Oh.' Well, that makes sense. I didn't think my father would have selected Critchlow and I hadn't seen any mention of it in the archives. That explained a lot.

'He and his men discovered that the Helenus, a rival organisation, was behind the break-ins. For years, they've only disrupted our operations and resorted to espionage, but Agent Critchlow is getting reports that they've recently scaled up and may be preparing something bigger.'

I feel colder all of a sudden. 'Who do they work for?'

'We don't know. We have our suspicions, of course; there are a few billionaires who would pay a lot of money to know... what we're discovering here, and rogue states who would likely ally with the Helenus to take control of the Programme. But so far, they've not succeeded.'

'Why weren't we told about this?'

'Agent Critchlow's men defend us. Our job is to focus on the science, the mission, the intelligence gathering. It would only have distracted and worried you, and in any case we could not give you any confidential information before your security clearance came through.'

The stark H against Tim's pale skin... H for Helenus, I realise, appalled.

'This is why I'm very concerned about what Agent Critchlow just told me.'

Uh-oh. Here it comes. Summary dismissal.

'Can you imagine what would have happened if this

Helenus agent had managed to lure you back to his flat?' I start visualising Tim without his shirt but stop myself.

'He'd have blackmailed you into joining Helenus.'

'Never.'

'Even if they threatened your mother's life?'

That gives me pause.

'Let's assume for a minute that you had not given in to blackmail. They'd probably have tortured you to obtain all the information you possessed about the Programme. And once your usefulness had been exhausted, they'd have disposed of you.'

I shudder, dreams of Tim's lips erased by images of torture.

'Olivia, do you understand the importance of the task at hand and quite how serious the Cassandra Programme's mission is?'

'Yes... yes, I do,' I stammer.

'Well, in that case, may I suggest you stop imagining that you have a future with the first passer-by and apply that very capable brain of yours to what needs to be done?'

Ouch.

'I will.' I stare at my hands, folded on my lap.

'Very well then. You can return to your day. Send me DeAnn, if you please.'

'Yes, ma'am.'

Did I just say ma'am? I groan internally and go in search of DeAnn.

As I look for her, a thought occurs to me: how did they know about Tim? DeAnn jogged past us earlier today, didn't she? She must have ratted on me. The cow!

12

DEANN

C*ambridge, United Kingdom, October 2016*

THEY'VE OFFERED me a post in the Programme's hospital, where I will study the data that the agents bring back from their missions. My role will be to make sure they don't bring back pathogens, to analyze any anomaly in their genetic makeup and deal with mishaps. A medical post, far enough removed from the field but close enough for me to learn what this is all about and turn a profit from it.

Olivia has accepted a role with the legal team where she'll deal with possible intellectual property and information breaches. Mostly, she'll ensure that none of the Programme's confidential information leaks to the wider public. She looked distinctly relieved to be offered that job and not the one we were actually interviewing for.

We're all going through the basic onboarding, but Björn and Andika, as they already had a high level of clearance, were vetted more quickly and they've been locked up in extra briefings for the last two weeks. Every time Björn and I cross paths, he looks stunned, green around the gills. I think he badly wants to tell me what he knows, but he doesn't, of course; he can't yet.

I'm making myself a smoothie in the kitchen when Snow White arrives, all agitated.

'You told on me!' she yells, visibly angry for the first time since I've met her.

'I have no idea what you're talking about.'

I pour the green mixture in a glass and start to turn away from her to wash the blender but she grabs my arm. I hate it when people touch me.

'Why would you do that to me?' There's a note of pleading in her voice even though she's furious.

'I was hoping you'd get expelled, of course.'

That shuts her up for a minute, her face the picture of incredulity and hurt. Her arm falls to her side and her eyes well up.

'Theodora wants to see you,' she says as she walks away.

I had a chat with Critchlow the other day and asked point blank why Olivia would ever be recruited into an organization like this one. He gets me. He's not like all these hand-wringing British people, he's American. I guess we're just more pragmatic and less sentimental because we're both outsiders and we don't owe any allegiance to her dead father.

Critchlow confirmed what I suspected; he can't understand either why Olivia was chosen. She's obviously out of shape, she's too emotional and can't hide any of her thoughts. She's putting us all at risk, especially if she starts blabbing about the Cassandra Programme to people who don't have clearance. She should be looking for a husband instead of coming to work for a secret organization. Maybe that guy who was about to kiss her will marry her, she'll push out a litter and forget all about the Programme.

I arrive at Theodora's office, knock and walk in.

'Ah yes, DeAnn, please come in.'

I take a seat in front of her desk, leaning back in the chair. The old woman is looking like an owl today. A beam of sunlight reflects on a deep indigo vase, giving the whole room a blue hue.

'Please explain to me the intent behind your actions today, DeAnn.'

'I just want to protect the Cassandra Programme and make sure that we only retain the best personnel. People who actually have the right caliber to understand the seriousness of the mission and who will put work before their personal lives.'

Her pale eyes are boring into me, over her lowered glasses. 'DeAnn, this is no longer a competition – you do not have to be better than Olivia, you're both part of the same team now.'

'I can't accept that. She's not qualified and she'll put our lives in danger. Agent Critchlow agrees, any of the other candidates would have been better. I understand that there also may be nepotism inv—'

She interrupts me with a raised hand, frowning. 'Olivia's father ran the Programme, yes, but that's not why she was invited to participate in the selection process. With your medical background, you must have realized by now that the MRI was looking for something specific.'

I remember the strange conversation I had with the consultant at the hospital and nod.

'We puzzled out that the brain configuration we're looking for is often hereditary.' She lets that sink in.

'Ah. Hence Olivia.'

'Yes, quite.'

'OK, fine. But all the candidates of the post-MRI rounds had the correct brain configuration as well. Plus, that's immaterial, now that we're no longer being considered for field positions. So why pick her?'

'You are getting ahead of yourself, DeAnn. It's not up to you to second-guess another staff member's worth and I should be grateful if you left the selection process to the Board. Who we hire and how we train them is none of your concern. This is the correct result. It's your attitude you should be worried about.'

'What do you mean? I'm acing the training.'

'*You* are the liability at the moment. You denounced Olivia to a third party. You are abrasive, unnecessarily competitive and are not behaving like a team player.'

I can't believe this, it's outrageous.

'If you cannot change your attitude,' she continues, 'your offer will be withdrawn. Do you understand?'

I cross my arms, annoyed at being lectured.

'As I said, you might have saved her life today. That's the only reason I'm not acting on this immediately. But I want to see a change, DeAnn.'

'Wait, what? I saved her life? From what?' It can't be the innocuous cardigan-and-satchel guy who was leaning in to stick his tongue down her throat, can it?

'There is something you should know...' She proceeds to explain the Helenus situation.

'Well, that explains the sedan that was following me a few weeks ago in Baltimore. I thought I was being paranoid at the time.'

She asks me for details but as I can't remember much else, she then instructs me to report all this in writing and asks me to work with Olivia and a sketch artist to describe the 'love interest'.

I get up and reach the door when Theodora says, 'DeAnn, you have one week to show me progress.'

My hand on the door handle, I nod and exit.

The Helenus, weird name. A quick search shows that Helenus was Cassandra's twin. These people sure like their Greek mythology.

I look for Bambi to start making it up to her but can't find her anywhere. Probably crying her eyes out over the dreamy boy or something equally ludicrous.

13

OLIVIA

C*ambridge, United Kingdom, 30 October 2016*

IT'S the end of the training, finally. I've found a mezzanine that's mostly used for storage, overlooking the dining room where they announced the results a few weeks ago.

From where I sit, the ceiling's wooden beams are close enough to touch. No one can see me, so it's become my favourite nook. Stacks of chairs and three-legged tables are strewn around the small space. It's so quiet that I can nearly hear the motes of dust as their golden dance ends gracefully on the floor. Bliss.

I'm reading the day's notes and jotting down questions when the sound of the main entrance door opening pulls me out of my reading. A slender, smartly dressed woman comes in, barely sparing her surroundings a glance as she walks briskly across the deserted reception room, heels echoing on the floorboards. She looks up when Andrew comes out to greet her but I can't see her face from above.

'Andrew, is everything set?'

'You didn't have to come all the way from California.'

'I did. You know I did.'

'It's not safe for you here. You shouldn't have come,' Andrew says.

'Yes, the latest missions have been... costly. You know what this means.' Not a question.

'One of us? It can't be. The fate of humanity is at stake here. Why would anyone betray us?'

'Andrew, we have a mole. It's time to face the facts and do something about it.' She sighs. 'Is Critchlow any closer to finding him?'

Andrew shakes his head.

'I'm glad you took my recommendation. I know Olivia's not an obvious fit but we need people who we can be sure will not betray us.'

I try to stay as still as possible; their voices drift up to the mezzanine clearly, so they could also hear me if I moved, thankfully neither of them looks up.

'Are you sure she's got what it takes?'

Ouch. Coming from Andrew, too.

'She's her father's daughter. You did the right thing selecting her, don't worry.'

'But she's middle-aged, out of shape, not particularly good at any of the security tests...'

'I expected better from you, Andrew. Do you really think that only twenty-year-olds with flawless bodies should be recruited? You know perfectly well that it takes more than brawn to make a good Programme agent. Observation skills, analytical subtlety, resourcefulness and an ability to blend in are just as important, if not more so than brute strength.'

'But in this instance, I'm afraid I have to agree with Critchlow's assessment; she's too keen to please, too naïve and guileless. She'll be eaten alive. She nearly got taken by the Helenus last week.'

There is a pause. It lasts a while. Long enough for me to start thinking that maybe this is my last day on the Programme. My heart sinks.

'You should be more concerned about DeAnn. I specifically told you *not* to hire her. What the hell happened?'

'Nigel insisted.'

She shakes her head. 'Alastair would be appalled to see what the Programme has become. Relying on Critchlow's agency is a mistake, he's gained too much power over the last few years.'

My pen slides out from my book and my sudden movement to catch it disturbs the dust, tickling my nose. No, no, no, I pinch my nostrils and sneeze into my bunched-up cardigan. Holding my breath, I listen to them but they don't seem to have noticed anything.

'... whatever happens she must never be allowed to become a field agent,' the woman says.

Who? Bloody hell, what did I miss?

Andrew hesitates. 'Of course, we're all grateful for the part you played in the Cassandra Programme and for your generous funding, but this is a very delicate time and we have to be sure...'

I see the slender woman put a hand on Andrew's arm. 'Spare me the bullshit, Andrew. The fact is that I'm the only one on the Board who's spent any significant amount of time in the field. You all have to listen to me, I had access to all the reports...'

'Maybe, but you know that anything could happen, that specific configuration might not necessarily occur...'

'Andrew, you don't understand, Olivia will di—'

McArthur appears at that moment and the slim woman stops talking. Andrew lets his objection taper out and they all leave the reception room together.

Jesus Mary Joseph, did she say that I could die? That's absurd, I'm just a lawyer, I'm in no danger. Am I?

14
DEANN

*C*ambridge, United Kingdom, October 31, 2016

BJÖRN, Andika, Olivia and I walk to the restricted wing in awkward silence, escorted by two security guards who leave us in a locker room. It looks more modern than the rest of the college, with its steel benches and narrow metal units. I've never been to this part of the building, so I glance around curiously.

There's a mission scheduled for tonight. As we've now all gotten our security clearances, the four of us are going to observe the agents' departure. Apparently it's rare for new recruits to see it. There are very few missions.

The two agents are already in the locker room, looking smug in their black flight suits; one is in his twenties, the other in his mid-fifties, both whitebread types with a can-do attitude. They're so picture perfect; they look like astronauts about to save us all from an asteroid.

Olivia, Björn, Andika and I pull ridiculous protective white overalls over our clothes. It's much harder to look smug in these but I try my best as I snap the rubber gloves on.

With the Helenus circling the waters, Critchlow's team is on high alert, patrolling the grounds with assault rifles in shifts. The atmosphere has been pretty paranoid since Olivia's fuck-up. Everybody's on edge and the sense of threat is palpable. Under the circumstances, it's hard to feel confident about the Programme. That's why I've decided to decline their offer. I'm leaving tomorrow morning to go back to Baltimore. I haven't told anyone yet.

The young, blond ersatz-astronaut is sitting on a bench, observing the four newbies gear up. Ankle resting on his knee, he looks relaxed but his armpits are stained with sweat. The older agent, his brown mop of hair shot through with gray, is standing apart, leaning against the wall. He's completely ignoring us, watching the backdoor, lost in thought, rolling a wedding ring around his finger.

I wonder why they're doing this. It's obviously extremely dangerous. They could end up as vegetables under my care; well, they might if I'd stayed. Personally, I'd be interested in studying their brains after the technology failed but I can't imagine that they'd like that scenario much.

And even if everything goes to plan, I understand from my soon-to-be ex-colleagues, the odds of making it back alive are quite low as the technology isn't exactly reliable. Why would they risk their lives? I guess that's what mainstream culture thinks heroes should do. Personally, I think they're stupid. And expendable.

Suddenly, yells erupt in the distance, followed by the thump of heavy boots.

'Did you hear that?' Olivia squeaks.

'Just an exercise probably,' I answer, shrugging.

Just as I close my mouth, an alarm starts to blare in the distance, followed by short popping bursts.

There's a loud crackling sound, and, as the older agent picks up the communication set, a voice calls for back-up; static garbles the communication and sudden screams are interrupted by a loud rattling noise. Then silence. Olivia's frozen, her pupils so dilated her eyes seem black.

The older agent fiddles with the radio button and all of us gather around him, staring at the radio when the back-door opens, slamming against the wall, making me flinch. Professor McArthur barges in, her usual composure frayed by urgency.

'Hurry, this way!'

Andika's already in motion. The rest of us rush after her and McArthur closes the heavy metal door behind us and locks it.

An enormous glass pyramid towers in the middle of the hangar and all around it, monitors, screens and dashboards are blinking madly. A siren shrieks, drowning the alarmed shouts of the Programme researchers who are getting up from their chairs, gathering their papers.

'Are they close? How much time left?'

'Quick! Move it along!'

'This way! Bring the burn bags.'

Dozens of scientists are already dashing from their work stations to shredders and back, removing armfuls of folders and laptops, desperate to destroy their work before our attackers breach the locked door. An Asian woman falls in her hurry and papers fly over the floor as she sprawls. She gets up on all fours, gathers her laptop to her chest, then fumbles with the papers. A colleague rushes to her side but instead of helping her up, he grabs her computer, removes the hard drive and smashes it to pieces.

'Disposal container at the back, quickly!' he shouts.

She picks up the ruined hard disk and hobbles to the back of the hangar, her knee bloodying her white overalls as scattered papers and one of her blue shoe covers are left behind on the floor.

An armed guard shoves me aside to check that the locker-room door behind my back is securely shut; then, holding his gun in both hands, he runs to the only other exit, on the opposite side of the huge area.

Maybe I can still get out that way. I sprint across the room, past the monstrous glass pyramid and over to the open door, to try to escape. As I run, I see one of the guards hauling a scientist to his feet, the old man's tufts of graying hair plastered with sweat against his shiny head.

'No, no, I can't. Just five minutes, this is twenty years of research!' The scientist stares at his screen, eyes wide, his Adam's apple visibly bobbing, but looking determined. 'Can you imagine what would happen if these thugs got their hands on it?'

'Just fucking RUN!' The young soldier yanks the researcher by the arm and pushes him toward the exit.

I tag close behind the balding man and pretend to be part of the team, as the armed guards gesture for our group to hurry through the door quietly. There's five of us or so. Glancing over my shoulder at Olivia and McArthur, who have remained near the pyramid, I sneak out and follow the soldier leading the cluster of scientists down a white corridor lined with identical doors.

My insides churning, I don't know whether to take the lead or hang back. The others are distressed too; the old man shuffles as fast as he can, his breath ragged as we all run in starts and stops and a young blonde woman cries incessantly, limping at the tail end of our bedraggled group. Fear and adrenaline course in my veins, distorting everything; the cramped corridors seem to become endless, and the tears that bathe the young blonde's cheeks make her face look like it's melting in the stark fluorescent light.

When we reach a bend in the hallway, the soldier skids to a halt and holds his arm up, so we stop. The old man bends, hands on knees, puffing. The young woman sits against the wall, wiping her face on her sleeve. I fight to stay still, itching to push them out of the way so I can escape from this underground maze.

The guard rounds the corner carefully when suddenly the rat-tat-tat of a machine-gun erupts, deafeningly loud and he staggers backwards as bullet holes burst through his chest. I forget how to breathe, frozen with terror. The young man slumps against the wall, a look of surprise on his face. His body slides down, leaving a bright red trail on the white surface.

The old scientist cowers with the others, as soldiers wearing balaclavas and black uniforms appear and step over the guard's dead body. They're turning the corner, machine guns held against their shoulders, aiming right for us. The young blonde scientist stumbles, unable to get back on her feet in her panic. She's the first to get hit.

The young woman's screams pierce through the tinnitus and before I've even made the decision, I've doubled back and I'm running. I falter and catch my fall, heart flailing. Behind me, screams explode and a thick smell of blood and cordite fills the air as I hurtle along the endless parade of doors, down the white corridor, panicking about missing the right exit. My lungs burn, my legs feel like they're not attached to the rest of me. I risk a glance over my shoulder.

They're catching up. Bodies sprawled. Blood. Others, fleeing from the attackers too. I run.

There! The right door. The Programme guards are closing it. Lungs on fire, I sprint faster, screaming, and they hesitate. I burst through as they slam the heavy metal door shut behind me, swivelling the large hand wheel and lifting the handle up.

Bangs on the door.

The cries of anguish rise to a crescendo.

Yells pierce the thick door, disturbingly clear and heart wrenching. A few seconds later, machine-gun fire erupts outside, each burst reverberating inside my skull. Then silence.

Bile rises in my throat. It could have been me. A stitch pinches my side as I struggle to regain my breath. No way out. We're trapped and there's no help coming. The guards step away slowly, jaws squared, aiming their guns at the locked gate.

'Back up, back up,' one whispers to me with a sharp head movement. When we've put fifteen feet between us and the door, we crouch behind a desk to regroup. The oldest one seems to be the leader, he rubs his stubbly chin worriedly, leaving a dark smudge on his left cheek.

'Charlie, how many extra mags left?'

The youngest guards looks scared. He runs a shaking hand through his blond curls, as he checks his belt, then holds one finger up.

The two older guards exchange a grim look. One of them holds his hand out and Charlie gives him the magazine. He looks so young.

'No one comes through this door, rookie, you hear me?'

The young man swallows and nods. The door is solid metal, several inches thick, maybe it will hold.

A heart-stopping thud startles everyone. All eyes turn to the far entrance. The attackers have reached the locker room on the other side and must be trying to ram it open. The sound reverberates in the large room, each bang like a clap of thunder. I flinch each time the metal door groans under the onslaught. Death is knocking.

We're surrounded. There's no way we can escape now. Fuck. I don't want to die.

The two older guards leave Charlie and me to it and rush over to the locker room door where they start piling up desks and chairs with Björn's help.

Charlie flinches every time a bang shakes the far door but I help him to drag furniture to our makeshift barricade and soon the two agents who were slotted for departure today come over to help us. I need to get away from the door, in case the attackers manage to break in. We can already hear them shooting at the thick metal on the other side.

I dash back to the pyramid. Maybe Professor McArthur will know a way out. Standing by the huge contraption, only two scientists remain entombed with us and they're grouped around the Professor, arguing in whispers, pale faced. It's the Asian woman with her bloodied knee and the guy who helped her with the hard-disk disposal.

I edge closer to try to listen in and spot Olivia as she hovers, hesitating, her face a frozen mask of panic as she looks toward each door. She flinches when another loud clang shakes the locker-room door.

The room vibrates with tension and the smell of fear hangs, acrid, in the air. Clearly terrified, Charlie's still manning the right door with the two Programme agents while Björn and the two older security guards are standing in a semi-circle around the left door, piling furniture in front of it, as the metal screams under the battering ram's assault.

Andika sprints to the two older guards near the locker-room door and starts arguing with them. They shake their heads and try to send her away but she persists and finally they give her a handgun. Björn looks at her then at the fire extinguisher in his hands. Resigning himself to the less than adequate weapon, he rolls his shoulders back, spreads his legs and waits for the onslaught, a grim, determined expression on his face. Andika takes her place in the semi-circle of defenders and raises her gun, aiming at the locker-room door. Both exits are covered now. But how long can we withstand an assault with only four armed people against who knows how many intruders?

And that's when it happens. Andika points out something to the leader of the guards, he turns to look and she deliberately places her gun at the back of his skull and pulls the trigger. The gunshot echoes in the huge hangar as the man drops to the ground. There's still a dark smudge on his stubbly cheek but the rest of his face is a mangled mess of flesh and blood.

I scream and backtrack into Olivia.

'What happe—' she says, turning toward the sound. She doesn't have time to finish.

Andika hears my scream and turns slowly toward Olivia and me, gun aimed at us. My legs move of their own accord, backwards, away from the assassin; I bump into objects and keep backing toward the pyramid's bulk behind me. Charlie, the young guard, yells, 'Get out of the way, she's going to kill you!'

Andika's gun moves in a slow arc as her eyes skim reluctantly over Olivia and me and lock instead on the young man who is running over to us, waving his arms.

Andika fires. The bullet hits Charlie, who stumbles and falls.

'No!' I yell.

I can't see whether he's hurt or dead. He did this to save me. A lump of guilt and fear lodges itself in my throat.

'Charlie! You fucking bitch!' The guard's yells are tinged with rage as he shoots at Andika and ducks behind the barricade.

Björn fumbles with the extinguisher and lunges forward, bellowing and spraying thick white smoke. Smoke whirls around Andika, as Björn rushes toward her but she stays stock still and shoots, both hands on the grip of her gun.

She's aiming for the red cylinder in Björn's grip, when, with a dull thunk, she makes contact and the canister bucks and jumps in the Scandinavian's hands, like an out-of-control demon vomiting smoke. A suffocating mist fills the room and everything devolves into blind chaos.

Screams of pain tear the fog apart and the thuds on the other side of the metal door accelerate, like terrified heartbeats. Choking, I lift the neck of my shirt out of my overalls and cover my nose, as my vision blurs with burning tears.

Andika races toward the pyramid and takes cover behind one of the workstations as she shoots at the remaining guard. The sound of gunshots is deafening, like explosions bouncing against the walls, mixing with screams.

Björn is shrieking. He desperately tugs on a bright red piece of shrapnel protruding from his stomach, as viscera slide out of him, like blood-stained eels writhing on the floor. Olivia's leaning over him and trying to press his intestines back into his abdomen as he screams his head off. The guard who remains on our side of the hangar is still trying to protect the locker-room door. If Andika takes him out, there will be nothing to prevent her from opening that door to our assailants.

The guard emerges from behind the barricade and with a cry of impotent rage, fires erratically. Somewhere behind me, Andika shoots back in a short, precise burst.

Something grazes my cheek and my ear starts to burn. I touch my cheek and my fingers come back stained with blood. Shit, I'm in the cross-fire. I drop on to my stomach and cover my head with my arms, gagging on the smoke. As I crawl away from the line of fire, toward the spot where I last saw McArthur, the Asian scientist materializes out of the fog; she's hiding under a desk, a trickle of blood on her face. She's praying, eyes closed, face pressed against clasped hands. Blinded by the white smoke, I'm crawling past her when I sense someone running towards us.

I flinch at the sharp clack of bullets, disturbingly close. The older agent collapses mid-run, a few feet away from me. His head hits the ground with a thud and his breath catches in his throat with a wet rattle. A puddle of blood oozes toward me. The white and gold badge on his shoulder is soaked in it and blood drowns the small embroidered pyramid logo as the man gurgles and tries to cling to my sleeve.

I clasp my palm against my mouth to hold back a scream and the Asian woman and I crawl around him. Charlie's still wailing, his shrieks emanating from the dense fog like a gruesome melody against the beat of the metal drums. I recognize the younger agent's voice: 'Shut the fuck up, man! Give me your gun!' But Charlie doesn't shut up.

The fog feels alive with threat as Andika circles silently around us, like a shark that could emerge from the mist to pick us off one by one. An exchange of bullets explodes, once more heart-stoppingly close.

Charlie falls silent.

A precise burst. Another. Followed by the tinkling rain of brass.

She's picking us off one by one.

My stomach drops.

Only one security guard left now unless she already got to him. I haven't heard him in a while.

As we crawl in the general direction of the pyramid, I feel the hair rising on the back of my neck. A red streak on the floor appears through the smoke, so we follow it on our stomach and elbows and after a few minutes we find Olivia bent low, panting as she drags Björn to safety. She's located McArthur. The elderly woman crouches behind a workstation, shielding the remaining scientist behind her. Olivia drops to her knees and pulls Björn's head onto her lap. The Scandinavian is whimpering softly, his eyes unfocused. McArthur stares from Olivia to me. Then I see her make her decision.

She turns toward the huddled scientists and whispers instructions. The man looks startled and whispers protests, gesticulating silently toward the door to the locker room, but McArthur contradicts him and the shocked scientist straightens and nods. He hurries, crouching, to his workstation and does what the Professor asks as his colleague hurries to a nearby station.

McArthur grabs something that looks like a gun, gestures for me to follow and yanks Olivia off Björn, hauling her by the elbow. Her white overalls are splattered with gore. She lets herself be pulled, dazed. I dash behind them into the glass pyramid, as McArthur closes the door behind us locking the swirling smoke out. I skid to a halt and bend over, clutching my knees, panting.

'You're going ahead with the mission. We'll launch the countdown in a few minutes,' McArthur says.

'What are you talking about? The mission is over, your agents are dead,' I say.

'We need to get back and help Björn...'

McArthur lifts Olivia's chin up. 'Olivia, look at me. I owe it to your father to at least try to put you out of harm's way before I engage the emergency protocol.'

'But where can we possibly go? The room's locked and there's no way to escape!' Olivia grabs her temples, her fingers leaving red smears on her pale skin.

She's right; there's obviously no way for us to make it out of this place alive.

'What's the emergency protocol?' I ask.

'I must destroy the pyramid as soon as you're gone. You're leaving for a year, so if anyone survives this, they'll rebuild the device before you come back.'

'What? Destroy the... What are you talking about?' Olivia is clearly panicking, her eyes huge.

The inside of the pyramid smells peppery and metallic. Outside, the two scientists are arguing. The man is pointing at the unguarded exit when Andika emerges from the fog and shoots him. He collapses.

We stare at her as she walks toward us, her braid coming undone, dark red spatter all over her face. She calmly replaces the magazine on her gun. We're in plain view, in the middle of the fucking pyramid. This is it then.

But as she starts to take aim at us, the older guard, still hiding behind the barricade, shoots her in the shoulder, destabilizing her. Reluctantly, Andika turns away from us to face the gunfire. The young female scientist, huddled under her desk, cradles her keyboard, typing desperately as she sobs.

'Listen, both of you,' McArthur says, straightening up, 'there's no time to explain. The guard won't be able to hold back the attackers for much longer.'

McArthur yanks Olivia's bloodied gloves off. They drop to the ground with a splat; then she pulls back the girl's sleeve and unceremoniously sticks a microchip gun in her flesh, jabbing her with the sharp end and depressing the trigger.

Olivia yelps and as soon as McArthur has removed the gun, she slaps her hand on the bleeding wound, breathing fast, visibly shocked.

My heart beating wildly, fighting to maintain my calm, I offer my forearm to McArthur and she looks into my eyes while she inserts the chip. I can hear the sub-text: *you are in charge of the mission now*.

I nod silently in agreement.

McArthur hurries out of the pyramid, closing the heavy glass door behind her. She throws the microchip implanter to the floor and runs to her workstation giving the Asian woman a few brisk orders but we can't hear anymore through the thick glass.

Inside the structure, a light is starting to shine from the floor tiles beneath our feet. As the radiance creeps along the slanted walls, a low hum intensifies and the whole pyramid pulses in response. I watch as McArthur gestures, issuing muffled orders.

The Professor turns to look back at Olivia, tenderness and desperation etched on her face. And something else too. Maybe guilt. The humming inside the pyramid reaches a higher pitch as the chips in our forearms begin to radiate heat. Olivia cries out, looking at her forearm, and I know why; I can feel the same ember-maggot wriggling its way inside my flesh.

Suddenly, there's an explosion and a loud metal shriek. Hands on my ears, I feel the blast reverberating in my chest, and when I open my eyes again, the far door is hanging off its hinges. Andika's body lies a few feet away from the door, jagged shrapnel protruding from her chest. A man wearing a balaclava and an all-black uniform enters through the gaping hole, but retreats when the security guard fires a volley at him.

The guard, shielded behind the barricade, shoots again, when a couple of canisters are lobbed into the room. There is a flash of blinding light and my eyes water but I see through the tears that the young scientist has fallen to her knees, holding her ears.

The frantic banging against the locker room's doors ends with a crash of clanging metal as that other entrance is breached as well. A dozen men in black fatigues rush in. The muffled sounds and the smoke lend the whole scene an oddly dreamlike quality. The masked men point at the pyramid and rush toward us. Gunfire flickers through the smoke. Bullet holes pierce the structure, as whole glass panels shatter, clinking to the ground like glittering hail.

I look everywhere for McArthur, hoping to find her alive. She's on her knees, tears running down her face, tracing streaks of pink through a mask of gray dust. She strains to reach her keyboard and just as she does, a flash of white light brighter than anything I have ever seen rips reality apart.

15

DEANN

C*ambridge, October 31*

WRITHING ON THE FLOOR, my body wracked by spasms of excruciating pain, I feel like I'm burning alive. Tears of agony are streaming down my face but I can't wipe them. Cramps rips through my entire body like an electrocuting current, bending me in an arc, as my shoulders strain to touch the back of my calves. I'm paralyzed.

My heart beats out of control as my lungs seize. My fingers are bent at odd angles and my tongue is stuck to the top of my palate. Battery acid is running through my veins. The only thing I can do is scream as tears run from the sides of my eyes. Olivia's face, a few inches from mine, is contorted and feverish as she twists backwards too, squirming in torment.

Now, the waves of fire come and go, separated by only a few seconds. A few minutes later, the contractions come in shorter and shorter bursts that are more endurable and farther apart. I start to breathe a few heartbeats at a time between the surges of pain.

Panting, Olivia and I look at each other, braced for more. Her hair is plastered in strands to her forehead. She's ghostly pale, verging on green. Sweat runs in drops along my temples, down my neck, and every muscle in my body feels bruised.

Finally, as the pain subsides, we lie still for a long while, whimpering and gulping in the stale air. Then my teeth start to chatter and shivers take over, as the cold envelops my sweat soaked skin. I'm naked. So is Olivia. What on earth?

'Have you ever felt... anything like this?' Olivia stammers, her voice hoarse.

'No, never.' My voice sounds strange, lower than usual.

We're in a dark hangar and the lights are slowly flickering on with little fizzing sounds. This room looks like it's been disused for decades. Where are we? What did they do to us? We must have passed out, been abducted and now the people who took over the Cassandra Programme facilities have woken us up by some sort of electrocuting torture. I look for other signs of mistreatment on my body but all I can see are smears of dried-up blood, sweat and dust.

'Look, we're in a pyramid,' Olivia says frowning.

Struggling to sit up, I squint at the dark and now I see it too. It looks like ours but older. The copper has turned green and streaks of grime stain the glass panels. The floor is dusty and the room smells of mold.

What the hell is this place? A rival organization's failed pyramid experiment?

Just as we get off our feet, a siren starts to blare in the huge hangar and flashing lights bathe the room in eerie red. I clamp my hands over my ears and struggle to get up.

My knees are unstable but I manage to stay upright. Pushing the dusty glass door open, I step cautiously out of the pyramid, looking around. The siren is even louder here, in the darkened hangar around the glass structure. The strident wailing bores through my skull, rattling my teeth and perforating its way through my palms into my eardrums.

Despite the noise and flashing red lights, there is no immediate danger, so I go back inside the pyramid and pull Olivia up roughly by the arm.

She gets up slowly, looking wobbly. 'Don't worry about me, give me a second. Is McArthur OK?'

I can barely hear her above the alarm. 'Olivia... come on, get it together. We're not in Kansas anymore.'

She looks at me, uncomprehendingly.

'What do you mean? We're not in Cambridge? How did we get here? Who took our clothes?'

I pull her out of the pyramid and walk over to the hangar's only exit, a small locked entrance on the far side with an intercom next to it. A few minutes later, the siren stops and then the sound of running footsteps and jingling keys reach us as doors are slammed somewhere close by.

Standing in front of the exit, I adopt a fighting stance, feet shoulder-width apart and glance at Olivia; she's hiding her breasts with one arm as she bends over to conceal herself.

'Olivia, you need to pull your shit together, STAT!'

What was I thinking? She's gonna be no help at all in a fight, of course but anything's better than trying to take on an unknown number of assailants on my own.

I sigh, turn to the door and roll my neck from side to side, but still the door doesn't open.

A loud crackle on the intercom makes us both cringe.

'Identify yourselves!' we hear through the static. I walk over to the intercom by the door and press the button.

'Who are you? Let us out of here.'

'How did you get in there? This area is highly restricted. How did you breach our security?'

That guy doesn't seem to know anything. Maybe we can take advantage.

'We didn't break in.' I hesitate. 'We're Programme agents.'

Olivia looks at me, her eyebrows raised.

There's a long silence on the other side of the intercom.

'Name, identification number and… date of birth?' says the voice.

'DeAnn Carpenter, ID number 2016M317, date of birth 16 September 1973.'

'Olivia Sagewright, ID number 2016L318, date of birth 20 July 1974.'

All is quiet on the other side.

The silence goes on for more than five minutes and my stomach starts to roil; I wipe my forehead with the back of my hand, unable to stop looking at the locked door. It was the wrong thing to say. The Programme facility has just been taken over by the military or by the Helenus. What if they're the same people on the other side of that door and are about to kill us? We have no idea where we are. We're not trained agents; we know jack shit about the situation. Olivia and I look at each other, her eyes are wide and she's worrying her lower lip.

He didn't buy it. I start running my fingers along the door, looking for hinges or a release mechanism of some kind.

Olivia must have come to similar conclusions as me because she starts walking around the pyramid, buck naked, frantically looking for another exit. But there isn't any and there are no windows.

Soon she's back next to me, scrutinizing the closed door, her chin dimpled with repressed tears. I wish I had a weapon of any kind or even shoes, so I could run at least.

There is a commotion on the other side of the door. Then the lock clicks and the reinforced steel bars inside it clank and groan as the door swings open slowly. A guard comes into view; he pushes the door wide toward us and then jumps back to point his gun at us. His too-thin frame is drowned by his uniform. I don't recognize the insignia. Both of his hands are gripping the handle and shaking, as he backs away from the door. Pale faced, eyes wide, he's staring at our naked bodies and looks like he wants to apologize as his tongue moves nervously on his lips, revealing crowded teeth under a scraggly moustache. He releases his double-handed grip on the gun to wipe his forehead with his sleeve, then tugs on a strange plastic collar around his throat that seems to be uncomfortably tight. His uniform looks really odd too. The jacket is short, the bottom half way too tight. He rubs his palm on the pants, then puts his hand back on the grip.

'Sorry, could you – please, may I ask you to – keep your hands where I can see them?' he stammers.

I raise my hands up and look behind him. If he's alone I can take him. He doesn't look like he knows how to use his gun and he's so scrawny, I could probably overpower him. But before I can try, Olivia steps forward with a watery smile, one arm extended in greeting, the other across her breasts, hiding them as best she can.

'Hello, I'm Olivia.'

'Umh... hello, I'm Stu – I mean, Stuart, miss.'

He stares at her, no doubt noticing that she's a real

redhead. Her breasts are pushed up against her forearm and her curves are on full display; he blushes, shakes her hand, eyes averted and looks back up at her face, swallowing.

We don't seem to be in immediate danger, so I let my fists down and move toward the exit. He steps in my way, looking embarrassed and awkward.

'What are you doing? Stop! I can't let you out.'

I'm not about to let him lock us in again. He looks weak, so I go around him and step out the hangar. He swivels, spluttering, 'Wait, wait, no get back in there, ma'am, please. You're not allowed. It's not proper process.'

The corridor is lined with doors on either side, with no clear indication of a way out. The paint is gray with age and flaking and there's a faint smell of mold and dust. We're probably in a disused basement. He's still pointing his gun at me, looking unsure, sweating profusely. If he raises his arm again to wipe his face, I'll take his gun, I learned the maneuver in Krav Maga. I don't recognize the make of the weapon and come to think of it I've never seen one like that, but I should be able to figure out how to use it. Anyone other than Olivia would take advantage of the fact that his back is now turned to her, to overpower him. But no, not Snow White.

'Stuart, we've had quite an arduous journey to get here. Is there anywhere we could sit and have some refreshments while you figure things out?'

Olivia sounds like she's at a fucking tea party. I sigh but let it play out.

'Yeah, yeah, sure.'

He leads us to an abandoned room, sparsely furnished with two scruffy sofas and a rickety coffee table. Every surface is covered with a gray coat of dust.

'Bring us clothes, water and something with sugar. Also

we need to talk to someone in charge.' Trying to match Olivia's non-threatening tone, I force out a 'Please.'

'Umh. Sure, OK. I'll bring you that. I already pinged the guv and he's gonna send instructions asap, ma'am.'

'That's brilliant, thank you very much, Stuart, we appreciate your help.' Olivia smiles. But when he leaves the room, she takes a big shuddering breath and exhales slowly.

He comes back a few minutes later with a uniform like his, water bottles and a handful of snacks. There's only one set of clothes, so I put on the tight pants and t-shirt, and Snow White gets a pair of boxer shorts and the gray synthetic jacket which smells of sweat. It's a really odd uniform, cut strangely. Apparently he didn't have any spare shoes, so we both remain barefoot.

Apologizing profusely, Stu leaves while we get dressed, visibly relieved not to make any decisions anymore. Why do the British always apologize? It's exasperating. As soon as the door closes behind him with a click and a light buzzing sound, I get off the sofa and look for a handle but there is none. I push the door with my shoulder. Locked.

There's a blue pad next to the door but I don't know how to use it to open the door. There are no intercoms or phone, no doors to anywhere else. If only there was a window, we could at least figure out where we are, or try to break it open. But no such luck.

Whoever took control of the Cambridge facility now has our lives in their hands. But how did they capture us and why can't I remember it? We must have fainted when that white light exploded. Maybe that was a stun grenade or something. At the first opportunity, I should escape. Leave Olivia behind. She'd slow me down and I don't want to be responsible for her. She can play nice if she wants to, but I need to survive.

'Nothing usable here,' I say, slamming my palm against the door in frustration.

'Nothing here either.' She's sniffling while she looks in some metal cupboards and opens drawers, the uniform jacket so short that it exposes the boxer shorts every time she bends to look down.

'Let's rest then, since we can't do anything for the moment,' I sigh.

I twist off the cap of my bottle and drink a long gulp. At least it doesn't seem like we're in immediate danger. I drink the rest of my water and think. There seems to be a hierarchical structure and the night guard doesn't appear to have instructions to kill us on sight – so far, so good.

Olivia drinks some of her water and cocking her head to one side, frowns. 'Is your hair different?'

My hands fly up and pat my cornrows. Feeling exposed and puzzled, I gather the leave-out and braid it, wondering why anyone would bother to remove my weave.

'Do you think we're safe?' she asks.

'We'll know soon enough.' I rip open the protein bar before she can get it and bite a chunk off.

'We should have killed the guy and taken our chances. Too late now.'

She looks shocked. 'Why on earth would we hurt Stuart? He hasn't done anything to us.'

'Seriously? Because we've been kidnapped and we have no idea who these people are, that's why.'

'Yes, but Stuart didn't seem to know much and I don't think he meant us harm.'

'Yeah, or he's with the Helenus and you're exhibiting the first signs of Stockholm syndrome.'

She taps the bottle cap against her lips. 'Stuart doesn't look like the kind of guy the Helenus would hire.'

'Neither did your dreamy history teacher.'

My words sting, but she nods. 'OK, maybe you're right, we should assume the worst then.'

She looks completely out of it. She rubs her face in her hands and the dried blood on her temples crumbles and scatters on the uniform shoulders. She hasn't noticed, she's staring curiously at the candy bar wrapper.

'That's odd, I don't recognize this brand.'

'Olivia, focus for God's sake. Who gives a flying fuck about the food quality?' I take a breath and make an effort not to snap at her. 'The Helenus took over the Programme; that much is clear. So we're probably in one of their facilities.'

'I'm not sure. If these were Helenus people, they would have killed us already.'

'They still might.'

'But why go through the trouble of abducting us and removing all our belongings?'

'Maybe they didn't want to take the risk that any of our clothes or devices might be tracked?' I venture. That reminds me. I check my forearm for the microchip. It moves under my skin when I push it tentatively with my grimy finger. Still there. None of this makes any sense.

'I'll take the first shift,' I say.

We both take a sofa. Olivia sleeps within minutes and I sit up, trying to fight my heavy eyelids. Now that the adrenaline has left my system, exhaustion takes over.

16

DEANN

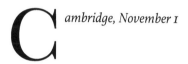

C*ambridge, November 1*

A HAND IS SHAKING my shoulder.

'Ma'am? Ma'am?'

I open my eyes blearily.

'Mmh?'

'My guv has arrived at HQ, we need to go.'

Stuart is bending over me, his gaunt face apologetic but excited as well. I was fast asleep for what feels like hours. Olivia's waking up as well. The stupid woman dozed off on her shift. She's useless. Well, at least they didn't kill us in our sleep, that's something.

Olivia is pulling back her hair into a messy knot.

'Ready?' Stuart says, looking at his feet.

He takes us down the corridor on the right and we start a long trek past at least a dozen doors. The walls are gray, paint is peeling off and the doors are all closed. It looks really similar to the Programme facility, but then again, so would any corridor lined with identical doors.

We reach an underground parking garage and all of us climb into an odd-looking minivan with smoked windows; Stuart sits in the front and says something really quietly and the clear plastic collar around his throat pulses with white light for a short instant and we set off.

We drive for the better part of an hour and I keep searching through the dim windows for a landmark or a natural feature that could tell me where we are, but come up empty. Ugly suburbs give way to high rises and clusters of uninspired project estates. It's all steel and concrete as far as the eye can see. We could be in any city. There is decay everywhere, the houses are grubby with dust and pollution. The roads are full of potholes and there's a yellowish smog hanging over the urban landscape.

Soon, we arrive in a downtown area where towers rise up to unfathomable heights, throwing long shadows over gray streets. The sidewalks are extremely crowded. Maybe it's rush hour or something.

Cars zip past our minivan, as we start to slow down and take smaller streets and finally we enter an underground parking lot and we all get out. Stuart guides us to an elevator. He calls out, 'Floor 186,' and waves his wrist in front of a pad.

'Where are we?' I ask.

'I'm real sorry but I can't say nothing. My guv will do the talking. Sorry.'

The lift is still going up five minutes later and my ears are blocked. I yawn to pop them and notice Olivia and Stuart following suit.

Finally the doors open with a ping onto a large reception area with lime-green carpets and stark lighting.

The PA, a thin woman in her fifties, looks at us with rounded eyes and quickly rises to escort us. She has more makeup on her face than I put on in a year. She's wearing hot pink leggings made of shiny spandex, vertiginous heels and a short faux-leather perfecto jacket. Her neon-pink wig is fashioned into a bird's nest held together by too much hairspray. Her face is pinched and her bright lipstick has sunk into the little wrinkles around her mouth, making her look disturbingly as if she's just eaten the chicks that might have lived in her hair's nest. What the hell is this place?

She opens the double doors and ushers us in like a show hostess. The whole place smells faintly of chemical deodorizer. We step tentatively into a vast office with floor-to-ceiling windows, as the double doors close behind us. Stuart, Olivia and I approach the walnut-burl desk near the windows. The green carpet feels thick and soft under my bare feet.

A man is standing with his back to us, surveying the view. The light is much more intense here, and, after the darkness of the underground floors, I'm blinded. I can't recognize this skyline at all. The city is covered with immense skyscrapers. The one we are in seems to be merely in the average range.

I search for something familiar and spot a river, but I can't really say where we are. It's got to be Asia. Where else would they build such high towers? Maybe a Gulf state?

My eyes adjust gradually, as the man turns to look at us. He has brown hair, very short on the sides and longer on top, gel slicking down the longer strands into a neat pompadour. His nails are manicured and coated in a dark gray polish. He's clean-shaven and also wears a full face of makeup. He's dressed in a weird outfit, a long jacket over a white t-shirt, no tie. His tight, shiny black leggings are uncomfortable to look at, so I focus on his silver sneakers.

He looks us up and down in silence and I'm uncomfortably aware that I'm wearing Stuart's hand-me-down uniform, which probably looks ridiculous on me. He turns to the hapless night guard.

'Rank, job title and name?' His voice is deep and I recognize the ring of command.

'Junior attendant, night shift of the decommissioned Cambridge device, Stuart Gainer.'

'Have you confirmed their identities?'

'Their name, rank, ID and dates of birth match two agents who went missing on the thirty-first of October 2016, boss.'

Well, yes, of course, that was a few hours ago, why even mention it?

'Have you scanned their microchips?'

'No guv, but I can do it now if you want.'

'Proceed.'

Stuart turns to us. Biting her lip nervously, Olivia extends her forearm and he scans her with a small, clear plastic device around his wrist. It pulses with blue light after the swipe above her forearm but nothing bad happens, so I extend my arm too.

'Their microchips match the two agents' IDs, guv.'

Technically we're not agents at all. Just back-office personnel. I say nothing, though.

'That will be all.'

Stuart nods and turns to us, looking unsure.

'Goodbye, Stuart, thank you for your help earlier,' Olivia says, patting his shoulder.

'You're all right,' he answers with a small smile. He hesitates. But after a beat, he turns and leaves. I see her throat bob as her eyes follow him to the door. I'm nervous too. But I won't let it show either.

I've kept my eyes on the older man during the exchange. He seems powerful yet also uncomfortable. I wonder why; after all, he's got all the cards here. He's the one who abducted us. Something's off. And what's with the makeup?

He sits at his desk and gestures for us to take the two chairs in front of him. 'Pardon the formalities, I needed to check that you really were who you said you were.' His eyes are cold and the apology rings hollow.

'I trust this is in order now?' I ask.

'Yes, it is.' He sits back and makes a steeple with his hands. 'My name is Montgomery de Courcy, I run the KEW operations.'

'What is this place? Where are we?'

'We're at the Programme headquarters, and today is the first of November 2081,' he looks at his wrist, 'and it's six a.m.'

The whole room seems to list off kilter. Resisting the urge to hold out my arms for balance, I grab my knees and try to get my beating heart under control. It can't be.

Olivia sucks her breath in and her face goes one full shade paler. Her knuckles are whitening around the armrests.

We look at each other.

The room still spinning around me, but I make an effort to keep a blank face.

The silence stretches as de Courcy observes us attentively. I swallow and cross my legs, trying to look confident while my mind plays catch-up. We left on 31 October 2016 in the late afternoon. Sixty-five years later, to the day. This is incredible. I thought I'd guessed what the Programme was about but I wasn't even close.

'Sorry, which city are we in?' Olivia asks, sounding winded.

'We are in the conurbation of London.'

My mind is scrambling to make sense of this. Could this be a prank? Or maybe a hallucination? I take a big breath and try to corral random thoughts into a semblance of composure and calm. OK, we're in 2081. We're probably in the hands of whoever took over in 2016. We're not agents, we weren't selected, we weren't properly briefed. Basically, we're fucked.

De Courcy's guarded, careful of what he reveals.

'So I gather that you were not expecting us?'

'You're the first Programme agents to ever arrive from the past. The room you appeared in and in fact the entire Cambridge facility has been out of use for twenty years.'

'I see.'

I take a moment to think. If this is the future, how come he's not asking about the attack on the Cambridge facility and the role we might have played in it? Shouldn't there be a report from whoever took control after the attack, warning any future heads of the Programme that two staff members escaped and might appear in their timeline? Or maybe he already knows exactly who we are and that's why he doesn't need to ask. We're dead if he's with the Helenus.

'Is this a Cassandra Programme building?' I ask. Not much point in playing coy.

'We're a fully operational time-travelling facility. We host all agents here and use a more modern pyramid for our forward missions.'

Again with the vagueness. Is he avoiding the word 'Cassandra' on purpose? His face reveals nothing of his thoughts and he leans all the way back in his armchair, observing me.

Whatever the situation is, we really don't have much of a

choice, as our lives are currently in his hands. I'll play along for now until I find an angle I can exploit.

Olivia has been watching me and when she sees me relax my posture, she breathes a sigh of relief and breaks into a smile. 'Thank you, Mr. de Courcy, for putting our minds at ease.'

She probably doesn't believe in evil and duplicity. I suppress an eye roll and try to match the idiotic expression on her face. I'm not so easily lulled, but for now, I allow him to think that Olivia speaks for both of us.

'Do you have a process for us to follow?' she asks.

I let her engage with him while I observe him.

'Yes, we've searched our archives for 2016 procedures and found an old protocol, which I read on my way here. We're assuming your microchip is programmed to return to 2016?'

'Yes, exactly,' I say.

Olivia looks like she might cry. I touch her bare foot with mine, as discreetly as I can. She turns to me and mirrored in her eyes is the same relief I'm feeling right now. We can go back. We can go back.

'Excellent, so we'll make sure to get you to the pyramid on time, one year from now, on the thirty-first of October 2082.' He smiles. His teeth are so white they're practically shining.

'Of course, the one-year mission,' Olivia says and I kick her foot again, harder this time.

'I'll see to it that you are back here in plenty of time. The protocol involves sending you to two countries, for a period of six months in each. You'll be together and accompanied by a Programme operative, so you can receive support when needed. The aim of the process is to ensure you gain an understanding of our timeline's situation. We'll

provide you with IDs, jobs and transport to your desti-
nations.'

That sounds good. Maybe this is going to work out
better than I thought. The only wrinkle is that we're not
actually agents. He doesn't know that and I'm certainly not
going to disabuse him of the notion.

'When you are in the field, you are not to intervene in
anything.' He stops and looks at us, clearly a warning. 'You
are to observe and only participate in activities related to the
jobs to which you've been assigned. I've summoned my
team and they've already started organizing the relevant
logistics. You should be able to depart in thirty-six to forty-
eight hours.'

'Thank you, we appreciate your support,' Olivia says
cheerfully, but she's chewing her lip.

'I'm arranging for the various specialists to brief you, so
that you'll have all the relevant information before you
leave.' His answers are frustrating. Seemingly informative
but also vague... '*Relevant* information': does that mean he'll
leave some of it out if it doesn't suit him for us to know it?

'Is there anything specifically that we should know or a
message you wish to convey to our leaders in 2016?' Olivia
chimes in.

For the first time, he hesitates. He stops, pensive for a
few moments.

'Thank you for the offer. I'll think about it and revert
back to you before your departure.'

Then he resumes the easy flow of the remarks that
betray the fact he's prepared practically every word he's
saying to us. This man should be powerful enough to
improvise. Why does he feel like a puppet reciting pre-
written lines?

'Now, if you'll excuse me, there're logistical details to arrange, as you can imagine.'

We both get up and thank him. I extend my hand to shake his but he just lets it hang there. Puzzled, I take it back.

'I've arranged for you to stay here at headquarters with our other agents until you leave for the first half of your trip.'

In other words, he's arranged to keep an eye on us.

'Thank you.'

He moves his mouth silently, holding a finger to a plastic collar around his throat and then he turns back to the window, ending the interview.

The PA comes back in and guides us briskly through a maze of corridors. 'Well, you both look a right state, don't you? What have you done in Cambridge? Wiped the floor with your faces? I guess there's not much sense in expecting hygiene and decorum from people who lived practically in the dark ages, is there?'

She throws a side-glance at Olivia and I can't say that she's wrong exactly. Snow White's hair is matted, her skin is stained with dirt and sweat, and the uniform isn't exactly a good look on her; she's had to leave some of the buttons open to accommodate her curves and the boxer shorts are too tight and too short. We take the elevator and the PA calls out, 'Level five.'

This floor feels more residential; Programme employees and children are mingling, going about their day. Breakfast smells waft through the air and the hubbub of conversations now serves as background to the PA's chatter, whose name we learn is Blossom. Despite her age and flabbiness, she's not self-conscious about wearing her leggings, but the style is unflattering, her flat, wrinkled buttocks wobbling as she walks.

People are starting to notice us and stop to stare at our trio, whispering to each other and pointing, fascinated. It seems the news of our arrival has travelled fast. Olivia tugs on the bottom of Stuart's jacket, hugging her in all the wrong places, and walks close to the wall, staring at her grimy feet; but I tuck a braid behind my ear and lift my chin up.

Blossom continues at a brisk pace until we get to a metal door, flush with the wall. She waves her wrist against a blue panel and the door opens with a whoosh of released air.

We step into a dark gray corridor so narrow that Olivia's shoulders and hips are touching the walls, so she has to turn to get through. There are ridges and alcoves along both walls; in fact, it looks like the corridor is lined with cupboards, the size of fridges, stacked lengthwise on top of each other up to the ceiling. Soon, we reach a minuscule living room, the size of a parking space, where there's a small boxy sofa, cushions on the floor and the usual detritus that roommates leave behind when they congregate – empty bottles, wrappers and gadgets.

'This is where you'll be staying for the next few days,' says Blossom.

She shows us a bathroom on the left, which is like a cube of plastic with the molded shapes of a shower, a sink and a toilet. About a dozen people's toiletries and towels are strewn about and it's not exactly clean.

Blossom goes back to the corridor, absorbed in something on her clear plastic wristband; she checks the writing on the stacked cupboards against her bracelet and stops in front of two of the long rectangular boxes, one at floor level and the one above it at eye level. She swipes her bracelet against an oval shape in the plastic molding. With a small click, the oval recedes and slides open to reveal a capsule with a thin mattress and pillow that take up the entire space inside. There are white plastic molded shelves on the walls that run the length of the coffin-like interior. I stick a head in mine. It smells of disinfectant with a faint hint of new car. Olivia gets on all fours and has a look at hers.

'Don't know what you did to deserve the VIP treatment but there you have it: lots of common space, an en-suite bathroom and even state-of-the art pods with privacy doors and everything. You're very lucky.'

'Thank you so much, Blossom, we appreciate it.' Olivia gets back on her feet with a wavering smile on her lips.

'Now if you'd like to change into something more...' she searches for the right words, looking us up and down with pursed lips, '... more 2081, perhaps. Take an hour to get ready and then you'll have breakfast in the mess hall.'

I should leave as soon as the opportunity presents itself. But when I look at the door, I realize there are no handles.

'How will we get out?'

'Oh right,' she titters, 'I nearly forgot to give you your iModes.'

'Our what?' Olivia asks, tugging at the jacket again.

'iMode, love.' Blossom shakes her hand under Olivia's nose, showing her the bracelet on her wrist. Hers is about three inches wide, shiny and rainbow-hued. The shriveled-up PA opens a pocket in her magenta jacket and pulls out two small boxes the size of a CD case but thicker. She hands a box to each one of us.

The packaging is minimal but extremely well made and fits the devices perfectly. The boxes contain a sort of collar, a bracelet and an ear bud each. All three devices are made of transparent hard plastic, arranged in concentric circles, like ripples on a pond. There is nothing inside, no instructions, nothing at all. The devices are identical; they shine faintly, emitting a diffuse white light against the black packaging. The ear buds look like the pea-sized hearing aids that older people wear in our era. I shrug and put the ear bud on. The device starts to buzz and I feel a pinprick in my ear.

'Ow!' Olivia yelps. Same thing happened with hers, then.

'Oh bless,' Blossom chuckles condescendingly. 'Your iMode has just taken a drop of your DNA to ensure it's completely customized to you. No one else can wear it now.'

Blossom helps us clasp the collar around our throats; I slide a finger in to try to release its hold but end up making it feel tighter. I take a big breath and fiddle with the clasp but can't get it to loosen. I hate the thing already.

'Give it a command, go on,' Blossom says.

'iMode, open the door.' The collar is so tight against my throat that it moves with my skin as I speak. But it works; the door behind me opens with a whoosh.

'Perfect. You'll learn more uses for it later. Just stay here and I'll arrange for someone to come and collect you in an hour.'

She leaves the narrow corridor, walking sideways like a crab, and the door closes behind her, sending the scent of her sugary sweet perfume wafting toward us.

'Did you see how she was dressed? Wow, I really hope that's not fashion now. It was so revealing.'

Of all the things Olivia could be thinking about right now, she opts for fashion. She's so irritating.

Climbing the small ladder on the side of her coffin, I slide into my pod. There's a TV on the ceiling, above the pillow, and the sides are lined with shelves and cupboards. On one of the shelves, there is a set of towels, a bag of toiletries and a black version of Blossom's outfit – tight leggings and a waist-length jacket. The only small mercy is that there are flat shoes instead of the high heels she was wearing. They look like surfing boots.

'Head to toe spandex it is, then,' I sigh.

Olivia pops her head in my capsule, making me flinch. 'Our tastes are probably old-fashioned here. Think about it – if a fifties person came to 2016, they'd probably find our clothes hideously tarty.'

'I guess so.' I shut the porthole.

We take turns showering. As I approach the mirror, I suck my breath in at the sight of my hair, stripped of its weave. Apparently, only our bodies made the trip to 2081, along with any smeared organic matter on our skin, nothing else. I wonder if maybe the chip is the only foreign object that travels forward because it's inside us? In any case, I'll have to make do with my own hair. I haven't seen it properly in months. It's grown quite long, actually, under the weave, but it's graying, damaged and way too frizzy. I try my best to re-braid it and tuck in a few strands but it's a waste of time. And the inadequate shampoo and conditioner aren't going to help, I sigh.

The bathroom's thin plastic flooring ripples precariously under my bare feet. Holding out my arms to keep my balance, I make my way to the showerhead in a corner of the bathroom, wincing at the grimy floor. The drain is clogged with hair and there are soap traces on the flesh-colored plastic walls.

As I'm trying to find a way to turn on the water, I grumble to myself: 'How do I turn on this goddamn shower?' and just as I finish the sentence, the shower turns on and I jump back, startled.

Voice activated of course. That's idiotic. Why not just use

faucets? My iMode lights up with blue flashes in response to my commands. Probably registering my preferences or maybe billing me for the water, who knows?

The water gets everywhere, but there is a drain in the middle of the plastic room and all the water swirls out through it. The spray of water is very faint. It's more a mist than a proper flow. I try to crank up the water but nothing happens. I do my best and finally exit the plastic cubicle, frustrated not to feel completely clean.

I step out, grab a towel and go dry myself in my pod while Olivia showers.

'DeAnn,' she calls out, 'did you use up all the water?'

'No, it was like that for me too,' I yell back.

I struggle to get dressed horizontally, as I can't stand in the pod and can barely sit upright. The leggings are actually quite comfortable, they seem to encase the leg and also shape it. It's as if they react to my body and adapt. The jacket is alright as well; it's zipped on the side with multiple inner and outer pockets and a hoodie. It's made of a material I've never seen before; it looks warm, breathable and water-proof. The closest 2016 material I can think of is the neoprene of a diving suit. I caught a glimpse of Olivia's outfit; it's nearly identical, with tight leggings and a short jacket but in a different cut and colored beige.

I rummage through the drawers and find nothing, no hairbrush, no pen and paper, no water bottle. Nothing.

Olivia gets ready while I search, then I jump out of the pod and we both stand in the cramped corridor, trying to find how to lock our 'rooms.'

'Can you believe it? Sixty-five years?' she says.

'Yeah. Everyone we know is probably dead by now.'

'You really ought to be more positive, you know.'

I roll my eyes.

'What I don't understand is why they didn't know we were coming. I mean, if it happened sixty-five years ago, they must have had ample warning,' Olivia wonders aloud.

'Maybe our emergency jump didn't count as a proper mission and didn't get logged by whoever took over.' I don't add out loud, *or maybe McArthur destroyed the facility and everyone in it after we left*.

'Maybe there's a security mechanism to erase all data in case of a breach, or this is so far into the future that they forgot all about us.' She looks hopeful.

'Yeah, maybe.'

I keep quiet about another possibility too: We never made it back so we didn't write a report about ever coming here. That would also explain why they didn't know about us in advance.

Just as we reach the door, there's a knock and when I say, 'Come in,' it opens automatically.

A blonde pregnant woman is standing outside our door, smiling and looking ditzy.

'Hi there, ready for your tour?' She sounds like an overzealous waitress.

An intense-looking man in his forties is standing behind her, leaning against a wall, arms crossed, observing us from a few steps away. He's looking right past me, at Olivia. She's turned away from us, pulling on her top and freeing her mass of curly red hair from the collar with both hands in a practiced, fluid motion.

The blonde is gushing in a slight Canadian accent, 'Wow! I... I studied history... and you're from there... or rather then. How soop!'

Ignoring her, I get out of the cramped corridor and brush past them into the main hallway.

'Oh silly me,' she continues, 'I didn't even introduce us

yet. This is Captain Burke, he's a senior Programme agent, and I'm Madison, I'm an analyst; we're here to show you around.'

'Madison, it's nice to meet you, I'm Olivia,' Snow White says, extending a hand, maybe hoping to stem the flow, but it has the reverse effect.

'Oh wow! Yes, of course. I read up about you before I came here. Was your father really Alastair Sagewright? One of the founding members? That's so galactic!'

The man behind her smiles imperceptibly and lowers his head. When he looks up, his expression is neutral again.

We get out of the room and follow Madison who keeps chatting, her face animated with enthusiasm. She isn't actually asking us real questions or waiting for answers, so I tune her out.

We follow the hum of conversation to a large mess hall where people are eating at long tables, sitting side by side. The smell of a breakfast fry-up hits my nostrils and my stomach gives a growl.

Madison gets served on a prison-style tray and when it's my turn, I get the same uninspiring fare: one egg, one piece of bacon, one sausage, one toast, a small glass of orange juice and a tea. Eyeing the disgusting-looking food, I try my luck with the woman in a hairnet who is serving us, while assessing the dubious cleanliness of her apron.

'Could I have an extra egg, some more toast and three more rashers of bacon? Oh, and where is the coffee? I can't find any?' I ask, feeling my stomach rumble again.

There's sweat on her upper lip and hairs protruding from it. She stares at me without answering, and exchanges a look with the next person in line, rising her eyebrows and muttering something that sounds like 'bloody foreigners'. The person behind me pushes me out of the way and gets her tray. Startled, I move along and, like everyone else, swipe my bracelet on a pad, receiving a ping and a blue flash in response.

We pick a table, sit down and dig in but when I take a sip of the 'orange juice' I nearly spit it out. It's disgusting: A thin, watery drink that's obviously chemical and has nothing in common with an orange except maybe its color. Trying to remove the awful taste, I get started on the fried egg and the bacon. The egg tastes normal but the bacon is vile, more like soy paste dyed with pink and white streaks. I gingerly try the bread. Normal.

Captain Burke observes us in silence. I notice the tips of a tattoo barely protruding from under his rolled-up sleeve. I remember Snow White's drawing of the Helenus symbol and wonder what the Captain's tattoos look like exactly. I guess I must be staring because our eyes meet and we evaluate each other for a long moment. There are deep lines on his forehead and his intense green eyes speak of a cold, calculating intelligence. Otherwise his handsome face betrays nothing.

I break eye contact, letting him have this small victory, and throw a glance over my shoulder at the queue, trying to decide whether to go talk to that woman again.

'Don't bother, she won't give you any,' he says.

'Why?'

He shrugs and wipes his plastic tray with the remaining bread, hunching over it slightly, as if to protect the food. 'You've used up your breakfast ration already. That's it, no seconds.'

'Your food allocation is assigned on the iMode, so no cheating,' the pregnant woman laughs, shaking her wrist. Under the stark neon lighting, suddenly the device doesn't look like a bracelet so much as a shackle.

I frown. 'Rations? You can't be serious.'

'For the last four years.' Burke pushes his tray away and leans back in his chair.

'But why are you rationing? I don't get it,' Olivia asks.

'Because we started to run out of food, of course.'

'Famine?' Olivia exclaims.

'Yup. You're not going to eat this?' Burke grabs the bacon on her plate and eats it.

'This isn't bacon, is it?' Olivia asks.

'No, of course not. Don't be ridiculous.' Burke laughs, a big throaty guffaw. He's one of those guys who hides his ruthlessness behind charm. He smiles a perfect white-toothed grin at Olivia, looking at her fondly like she said something cute.

'But how is this possible? Don't you have productive agricultural methods by now?' I ask. 'I mean, your technology must be miles ahead of ours. Don't you have high-yield crops and...'

'Technology can't always fix everything. There is food, of course there is. Just not enough for everyone.'

'Why?' Olivia asks.

Madison shrugs. 'Take your pick: climate change affecting farming, lack of GMO seed resilience, antibiotics resistance leading to mass livestock die-offs...'

Olivia and I look at each other as Madison continues to list the issues. Around us, the Programme staff are milling about, getting breakfast, chatting to colleagues, reading their iModes. It all looks so normal.

'I try not to think too much about these things. What can we do about it anyway, right?' Madison reaches for Olivia's glass of orange juice. 'You're not going to drink that, are you?'

Olivia shakes her head and we watch Madison down the whole thing, while rubbing her distended belly.

'Waste not, want not,' she says.

'Do you want mine?' I ask her.

She squirms in her seat and shakes her head.

17

OLIVIA

*C*onurbation of London, *1 November 2081*

SEVERAL PEOPLE ARE LOOKING at us. Nearly everyone here is wearing a version of our outfits in varying colours and fabrics. Most have the same type of jacket as we do, some are wearing tight t-shirts only over the leggings. I wonder whether maybe there's a dress code or is it that people are just so accustomed to wearing the same type of outfit all the time, for convenience, that they don't realise anymore how similar they all look to each other?

All the women here have very short hair, pixies or buzz cuts. Some have a side of their head shaved, and most have dyed it in outlandish colours: turquoise, orange, neon green. Some are just completely bald and tattooed with swirling flowery designs or busy geometric shapes. DeAnn and I stand out with our long hair, despite the shiny new clothes.

Madison is chatting away, explaining small things and

showing us how to access the bank accounts that Blossom opened for us this morning. The young blonde woman must have been sent to make us feel welcome. She speaks very quickly and tends to laugh at the same time. She's slender and has a beautiful face with long, rectilinear features. Her eyes are blue and although she wears too much makeup like everyone else here, she looks fresh somehow. Her bobbed hair is longer than that of any other woman we've seen so far, reaching just above her jawline. She smiles at me when she sees me staring at her round belly. I blush and avert my eyes, biting my lip.

'There's so much to talk about. Where would you like to start?' she asks.

'Is there a quieter place we could go?' I ask, as people are staring openly at us by now.

'Actually, we've been cooped up in here for hours. Take us outside,' DeAnn says. Madison hesitates and DeAnn presses on: 'We're not being held prisoner here, are we?'

'No, of course not.' She chuckles uncomfortably.

'Well, then.' DeAnn gets up, leaving her tray on the table.

Madison glances at Captain Burke. He nods.

'OK, follow me,' Madison says with a smile, as she gets up.

I gather DeAnn's tray and mine, feeling ridiculous in the unflattering spandex; I might as well be naked in the beige outfit and my cellulite is probably showing through the thin fabric. Wishing I'd gone to the gym more often over the last year, I struggle to get up from the bench and angle my bum away from view as I wait for the Captain to walk ahead with Madison and DeAnn, but instead he helps me put away the trays.

'Olivia, right?' He has a really deep voice.

I nod, blushing.

'You're not what I expected.'

Gosh, I bet he's used to people being fitter, with the rationing and all.

'We've never seen anyone from the past before. It's exciting.'

'What do you do here?' I ask.

'I'm an agent, just like you.' He smiles.

What? Oh right. For some reason everybody here thinks we're agents. Better play along.

He guides me through the building, chatting about inconsequential things, and I find myself relaxing. He has a warm laugh.

'So you travel forwards too?' I ask.

'Yes, I used to. Now, I'm more senior, I overlook a project to replicate the technologies we find in the future.'

'That sounds really interesting.'

'You mean boring, I think.' He smiles. His accent's polished but there's a faint cockney trace below the surface.

An escalator takes us down into a vast hall. The ceilings here are at least three storeys high and all along the lobby's glossy black glass walls, giant digital screens are displaying videos in what looks like Chinese, which the people passing by below assiduously ignore. The place is so full it looks like a pre-Christmas crowd in a commercial centre.

Diving into the flow, we head towards the exit. A few metres away from the revolving doors, we cross a line on the ground and each of our iModes beeps and flashes for a second. The security guard looks up and says something to his wrist.

Then we're out.

The sound and movement are completely overwhelm-ing. Throngs of people rush past us within centimetres of each other, ignoring each other in pure London style. Wearing spandex leggings in various colours, with transparent cut-outs strategically placed both to reveal and hide, most passers-by are not actually walking but standing very still on round, electric hovering contraptions. A few are zooming past on electric skateboards, scooters and bicycles.

Most people around us have their heads encased within glass bubbles that resemble overturned fish bowls. They look like they're talking to the air inside them, as though they're mad, yet everyone seems to find it completely normal.

The streets are milling with thousands of pedestrians, all jostling for space, pushing and weaving past us. The road traffic is whizzing past too; it seems that all the cars on the road are driverless and they're driving as one, as if the same programming were pulling them forwards.

Yet, despite the huge crowd and bumper to bumper traffic, the street is eerily silent, except for the rhythmic clapping of people's gummy shoes on the ground and the occasional whine of their small, round scooters. The cars are silent as well. It's unnerving to be surrounded by a crowd yet hear nothing.

I turn around and look at the building we left, rising up higher than the Shard. Buildings the same head-spinning size sprout everywhere, reaching up into the yellowy smog dome above us.

Dazed, I try to focus on specific people, as the size of the crowd is making my head spin. A group of thirty-something women in front of me are walking together, pushing prams. About half of them are pregnant and wearing multi-coloured leggings with tight tops that show off their round bellies. One of them has thinning hair and her pallid skin is dry and blotchy. A middle-aged woman, her red hair shaved in a buzz cut, chats away inside her bubble, pulling her toddler roughly by the wrist. He's wearing a breathing mask that's eating up half of his face, and is looking longingly at her, but she's oblivious. The thought comes unbidden to me *I'd take so much better care of a child if I had one*. My heart does a weird backflip and I bury the thought away. Above the rubber mask digging into his puffy cheeks, the toddler's blue eyes seem too wise for his age. I smile at him but the woman yanks him away, glaring at me suspiciously.

It all looks so normal at first glance and then not so much, like a familiar tune gone off-key. Although we're now in November, the weather is warm and humid, at least 25°C. As I look up to take in the overcast sky, I notice a white and green flag with a red cross overlaid on top. The building looks official; shouldn't this be a Union Jack? What's going on here?

The smell of rotten eggs abruptly interrupts all my thoughts. I pinch my nose and gag while we cross what must be the Millennium Bridge. The stench that's wafting up from the Thames is overpowering. It feels like I'm inside a dustbin lorry. Retching, I grab the bridge's railing and glance at the river; the water's practically gone, only a bed of mud and a trickle of water remain.

Madison and Captain Burke haven't noticed anything and are talking quietly, walking ahead of us. Captain Burke walks with a slight swagger, a hunching and tightening of the shoulders that speaks of roughness and modest upbringings.

DeAnn has removed her jacket and is pushing it against her face as she scrutinises the streets and canal pathways searching for something. I'm too busy trying to breathe through my mouth to ask what she's looking for.

People are streaming all around us, forming eddies

around our obstruction, too English to curse at us. DeAnn is oblivious to the dirty looks we're getting. Holding my sleeve against my face, I hurry across the bridge to catch up with our guides.

'I don't know what may seem strange to you. So why don't you just ask and we'll do our best to answer,' Madison says with a smile.

As we make our way along the Thames riverbank, I look around, trying to think of something to ask them. Most benches are occupied by elderly people in various stages of decrepitude. A short distance away, a gaggle of teenage girls is gathered around a transparent plastic screen, silently shrieking about a boy band video of some sort, their heads wrapped in the odd-looking fishbowls. Their hair ranges from mermaid green to dark purple and they're covered in colourful tattoos. Their cropped leggings barely cover their knickers, the bottom part of their bums clearly visible, hanging out of their skimpy, tight shorts. The effect is quite eye-popping. Don't these girls have parents?

'Is this an air filter of some sort?' DeAnn asks, pointing to the glass bubbles on people's heads.

'What? Oh no, no.' Madison chuckles. 'Wait, you'll see.'

She tries to touch DeAnn's neck but my partner jerks away. Taken aback, Madison turns to me instead; she touches my collar at the side of my throat and a screen appears in front of my face, startling me. It's transparent, so I can still see the waterfront through it but now a menu is superimposed on the crowd of people, with boxes of scrolling text in garish colours and flashing images that come and go. Madison and Captain Burke start walking again, so I follow them, trying to adjust to the extra layer of information that the iBubble displays. The whole world is muted in here and the only things that seem real are the colourful images popping up on the curved screen.

My ear bud is spewing out over-excited chatter and I can't find a catch on the collar or an off-switch either. Everywhere I look seems to activate a flood of information; from the special deals at this tech shop, to a passer-by's full bio and personal photos and a brothel's ad.

Panicking in the claustrophobic iBubble, as the sex workers start to pant and show me their lady parts, I tug at my collar until Madison takes pity on me and releases the catch. The iBubble retracts into the plastic band around my throat and we catch up with Captain Burke, who is answering one of DeAnn's questions as he guides us through the crowd towards a pub, which I unexpectedly recognise; it's the Founder's Arms. Heartened by the familiar name, I follow them inside, feeling as if I'd just found flotsam to hang on to, just as the mudslide of time was threatening to drown me.

We each order our drinks at a self-service machine and navigate a path through the enormous café. Hundreds of people sit at very small tables, so close they're elbowing each other. The multitude of people pressing me on all sides is exhausting.

Captain Burke takes one look at me and gestures to Madison, who guides us upstairs to a small room overlooking the river and the London skyline. From here we have a view on St Paul's which looks forlorn and grey, shrunk somehow, as it sits squished between towers that loom menacingly over it.

We sit and take in the view for a moment, each one lost in their own silence, relishing the luxurious privacy.

'We... Madison and I think there are a few things you should know... it's probably better if we tell you outside the

Programme premises. Are you guys too tired or can I go ahead and brief you?'

'Oh, that would be so helpful, actually. Thank you, Captain Burke.'

His lips stretch in a smile. He lightly touches my shoulder and I intensely wish I weren't wearing beige spandex.

'Please call me Anthony – and it's no trouble at all. If I were in your position I'd want to know as much as possible before going on mission.' He goes over to the door, waves his wrist in front of a pad and says, 'Maximum privacy.'

The glass walls all around us become frosted and opaque, and the sound quality in the room turn muted. Maybe soundproofed.

'So what do we need to know?' DeAnn's arms are crossed as she leans back in her armchair.

'You're being sent to Uganda,' Anthony says.

Madison sucks her breath in. 'Are you sure, Anthony? Has it been confirmed?'

He nods grimly.

Madison says, 'I don't understand why the Programme would risk your lives and send you there. I guess they want to showcase for you the main issue of the age in a country that will epitomise the problem... but still.'

'What's the main issue of your era – is it famine?' DeAnn asks. 'I mean, do we really need to go all the way to Uganda to figure out that there's famine in Africa?' she scoffs.

Urgh, the woman's so callous sometimes.

'Famine's not the main issue, that's the symptom,' Madison says, rubbing her pregnant belly.

'OK, I'll bite.' DeAnn frowns. 'What is main issue of your era, then?'

'Before I tell you, I guess there are a few things you

should know. First off, we've pretty much eradicated communicable diseases, so mortality has sharply decreased over the last three generations,' Madison starts. 'Life expectancy has soared as well and sits at around one hundred and twenty years old on average nowadays.'

'Wow, that's phenomenal.' DeAnn sits back in her chair. 'But it doesn't sound like an issue.'

'The medical advances are of course a positive development,' Madison continues, 'but it had an unintended consequence: we now have about four billion people over the age of sixty in the world. In Europe practically one in two people are senior and the over-eighties population has multiplied by seven since the year you left.'

Ah, so it wasn't my imagination, earlier, when I thought I saw elderly people everywhere.

'As a result, mortality rates are decreasing, child mortality in particular, is a thing of the past, and in parallel, most regions have continued to be quite fertile.'

'Why are you both so glum?' I ask, puzzled. 'Surely having amazing medical advances, living longer and ensuring babies survive into adulthood is fantastic?'

'Yes and no, Olivia.' Anthony shakes his head, trying to find the right words. 'We're faced with exponential growth in a finite environment. It's like trying to put two litres of water in a one-litre bottle. The Earth's carrying capacity is still the same as it ever was. But our population keeps multiplying, with no end in sight and it isn't sustainable.'

'But I don't get it,' I puzzle out loud. 'What's the big deal? So what if there are more of us? There's enough unoccupied space all over the world to accommodate more people, surely. I mean, Canada for a start is huge—'

Madison interrupts, 'It *does* matter that there are so

many of us. We're on the brink of exceeding the carrying capacity of our ecological environment.'

'Do you mean like Earth Overshoot Day?' DeAnn asks.

'Yes, just like that.'

'Earth what?' I ask, looking at each of them in turn, puzzled.

'Earth Overshoot Day is the point in the year when we run out of our allocated supply of natural resources,' Madison explains. 'Normally in any given year, from the first of January to the thirty-first of December, we should have enough supplies to feed and sustain the whole word's population. When we started calculating Earth Overshoot Day in the 1960s, we had a surplus of about three months. Then, in the 1980s, we could last until mid-December. In the noughties we ran out by October. In 2016, you started using the next year's resources in August.'

'I don't get it, so what?' I ask.

'Well, that worked only as long as the following year yielded enough. It's like living on credit and then losing your job. You can't pay back the money you've already spent, so your current survival as well as next year's survival becomes jeopardised. That's exactly what happened: our crops started failing and we ran out of food.'

Remembering how hard it was for Martin and me to conceive, I frown, wondering. 'Isn't fertility decreasing? Sperm counts are dropping in developed countries and I thought women just had an average of 1.8 children, below the generation renewal threshold. Isn't Europe's fertility nose-diving? What you're saying can't be right.'

'Yes, in a way, that was partially true. But humanity's numbers overall aren't decreasing. Our growth is just slowing down – and not fast enough. Each generation grows in size, which means the number of fertile women grows as well.'

'How is that?' I ask, feeling even more confused now.

Madison explains: 'Let's say three women had eight children each in 2016. By the time these children are twenty years old, there are now twenty-four adult offspring. Let's say that twelve of these are women who go on to have four children of their own each: that's forty-eight kids. You see where I'm going with this? Even having eight children each, the three women in 2016 had half as many babies as the total born to their twelve daughters, who have four each. So even though fertility per woman is decreasing, the overall population is still growing exponentially.'

'Oh, I see.'

'So now we face a situation where fertility is on average 2.5 children per woman in the world and approximately 3.5 per woman in the least developed countries.'

'We've just reached fourteen billion people on Earth last month. And we seem to be on course to reach sixteen billion by 2100,' Anthony adds, looking glum.

DeAnn frowns. 'So you're saying that the main issue is not really the availability of food, it's overpopulation? But won't famine lower these demographic projections?'

'Only about fifteen million people worldwide died of starvation in the last one. Sorry to be crude, but it's not even making a dent,' Anthony replies. 'You and Olivia are humanity's best hope at this stage. You're the only ones who can still prevent our catastrophic overpopulation or at least lower humanity's growth rate, so we never reach this point.'

He throws a glance at Madison's distended belly and her mouth slants downward as she rubs her bump, head bowed.

Anthony looks at his iMode. 'We should go back, we're going to be late for your assessment.'

We're subdued on the way back, each of us lost in our thoughts. When we reach the Programme building, Madison hesitates, then says, 'Listen, I'd really like you to meet my family. Do you think you could all come for Sunday lunch?'

'Yes, of course we'd love to,' I rush to answer before DeAnn can decline.

'See you tomorrow then.' The blonde woman smiles as she holds the lift doors open.

We get out and Anthony walks us to our next appointment.

18

DEANN

*C*onurbation of London, November 1, 2081

BURKE TAKES us to a part of the Programme building that we haven't seen before. It's deep underground and we pass through several rooms where soldiers are relaxing or attending briefings.

Everyone is dressed in fatigues here and there are a lot more weapons on display; guns on their belts, rifles being cleaned, knives strapped around thighs. This doesn't look like the Programme facility I'm accustomed to; it feels like a military operation. I suppose this was the logical evolution of the Cassandra Programme, if they had to protect themselves against external attacks like the one that happened yesterday. Or rather, sixty-five years ago. But still, it's jarring.

The vast majority of military personnel we cross paths with are men. They assess us as we walk past. Some have nasty-looking scars and no one smiles. Any one of these soldiers could overpower us at any moment. We have no idea who these people are, after all. None of the men looks very happy to see us.

Burke stops in front of a large door, I hesitate; he could be taking us to an interrogation room. I step in after him, on my guard, but it's only a gym. There are soldiers everywhere, lifting weights, looking at themselves in mirrors or watching a holographic projection showing them how to use a piece of equipment and replicate it. They're all muscular and fit and I like the room's intensity and drive, the relative silence only interrupted by grunts of effort. The smell of sweat and linoleum is familiar, so I breathe in and make an effort to relax.

Our guide escorts us to a small room at the back of the gym where a large muscular man, probably aged sixty or so, is waiting for us. He's wearing fatigues, his hair is white and short, his forehead is high and there are deep frown lines in his tanned face. He makes no move to welcome us; instead he gives us a once over, his hands clasped behind his back.

'Agent Carpenter, Agent Sagewright, come in.' His South African accent lends a clipped rhythm to the order.

There are mats on the floor, a few pieces of equipment and we're surrounded by glass, so it seems that our training will be on public display. I wonder if that's on purpose. They strike me as the kind of people who don't do much by chance. Burke closes the glass door and stands to attention behind us, waiting for instructions.

'You've already met Captain Burke and I'm Colonel Schalk Groebler. I oversee all Programme field operatives and you'll now report to me during your year here.'

Say, what now? We don't report to this guy, that's for sure. I stay quiet and exchange a look with Olivia, willing her to remain silent.

'This afternoon I'll brief you on the basic knowledge needed to survive during your mission. We'll then evaluate your level of fitness.'

Groebler looks Olivia up and down, his thoughts barely concealed; he obviously thinks she's a fat slob and not fit to be here.

Olivia crumples a little, the way she does when she loses her self-confidence. She crosses her arms, bends in the middle and angles her feet inward. My temper rises before I have time to think. What the hell? I'm feeling protective of Snow White, that's new. For the first time since I've met her, I'm actually feeling something like a partnership with her. She's the only one who knows that we're in over our heads. The only one on the planet, right now, who has any idea who I am and who cares if I live or die. I push down the knee-jerk protectiveness and force myself to keep a blank face.

'As Captain Burke is going to be your CO for the remainder of the year, we need to evaluate your field readiness in order to adapt our...' he looks for the right word and I wonder what he was going to say: monitoring? '... assistance to your needs.'

He makes a face, as if the last words had left a bad taste in his mouth.

Burke proceeds to test Olivia and me on basic self-defense and fitness exercises. I let Olivia go first. Obviously Burke takes control of her within seconds. She flops on the mat like a helpless bunny, her red hair spreading in a halo around her head. To her credit, she doesn't give up and thrashes to get up, but he's simply too strong. Burke smiles and holds her wrists down, pinning her with his hips. He stays like that longer than strictly necessary and a blush blooms on Olivia's face as he whispers something in her ear.

She gets up really fast, tugging on her tank top, and hurries over to sit back on the mat, next to me.

Once again, it occurs to me that we're in the bowels of a military building, surrounded by soldiers whose allegiance is unknown and that we have no idea what their end-game is. So I decide to play dumb and match Olivia's level of ineptitude. It takes every ounce of my self-control not to respond with the Krav Maga moves that my muscle-memory is begging to apply. Burke makes short work of me, he trips me up and instead of catching my fall, lets me drop to the ground and bends my arm against my back, holding it painfully. Cocky bastard. I yelp, taking on a more high-pitched voice.

'Ow, ow, my shoulder!'

As Burke gets up, he exchanges a smirk with Groebler.

Olivia is gawping at me in surprise and I shake my head quickly, as I take my seat on the floor next to her. She gets it and thankfully doesn't say anything. We continue in that vein for a couple of hours, Groebler running us through evaluations, Olivia failing naturally at everything and me doing marginally better but not by much. We've become quite the attraction, with a dozen agents gathered on the other side of the glass walls looking in and catcalling. More than once I nearly blow it and take over, taunted by their jeering. But I resist the urge to twist Burke's wrist and make him scream for mercy.

Finally, the onlookers tire of watching Burke kick our asses again and again, and drift away. Colonel Groebler stands at one end of the room and the three of us look up from the exercise mats; Olivia red-faced and discouraged, Burke smug and calm, me humiliated and silent.

'Ladies,' in his mouth the word sounds like a terrible insult, 'the level of operative skills you displayed here is a disgrace. That the Programme would risk your lives and more importantly that they'd risk all of *our* lives by sending amateurs here is...' He breathes hard and closes his mouth, his jaw working with the effort of staying calm.

Olivia looks at her shoes. He's right, of course. How on earth did our records get changed? We were never agents. Something is going on, but I'm damned if I know what. There's no advantage in telling him that we're back-office personnel, though, so I keep silent and wait for the rest of the dressing-down.

'Your fitness level and stamina, your physical condition,' he looks disdainfully at Olivia's curves, 'are below standard even for desk staff here, let alone field agents.' He turns to me, shaking his head with disgust. 'Your ability to defend yourselves against attack is nil, your knowledge of survival skills isn't enough for you to find your way out of a mall. Don't you realize where they're sending you?' Each word is hammered as he gets visibly worked up with each sentence. 'You're going to *Uganda*.' He makes it sound like the seventh ring of hell. 'This is a fucking joke...'

He takes a deep breath and tries to calm down, but a vein is bulging out of his neck as one of his fists punctuates each point he makes.

'Do you have any idea how they reacted when they ran out of food a few years ago? They started out by killing each other with machetes, that's how. Then they sent raiding parties to take over parts of Tanzania and Kenya. The situation there is back to a manageable level, but it's still a fucking mess. There's no water, no sanitation, little food and diseases are running rampant. They're all on top of each other like vermin.'

Vermin? So nothing much has changed, racism is alive and well, even on the eve of the twenty-second century. I'm not even surprised. He seems to have completely lost sight of who he's talking to. I mean, I'm African American for God's sake.

Burke clears his throat and Groebler snaps out of it. He takes a big breath.

'It is what it is.' He squares his jaw. 'We'll just have to... assist you as best we can.'

Again the hesitation.

He taps his iMode and the gym disappears, as the glass around us frosts over and a screen materializes on the walls of our small room.

'You've been briefed about the overpopulation issue, correct?'

'Yes, Madison...' Olivia starts.

'I bet she didn't tell you the whole story. Bleeding-heart leftists, all the same,' he mutters.

A world map appears on the glass panel in front of us. It's in 3D with countries glowing in different colors. The map is mostly green all over, except for most of Asia, which is bright yellow. The date '2015' is floating, superimposed at the top left corner of the map, revolving on itself and glowing against the Atlantic Ocean's light blue backdrop.

I get up to reach for the map and the display reacts to my iMode bracelet. As I touch Asia, a figure appears above the continent: 4.4 billion. I try a green one: Europe: 0.7 billion. Africa is green as well, I hover above it and 1.2 billion appears.

Groebler says something inaudible and the date's digital numbers start turning fast as the map goes from mostly green to red and amber all over. Finally, the date stops at 2081 and the map stabilizes.

Below my hovering hand, Africa is glowing bright red,

Asia is red as well; the Americas are amber. Only Europe and Japan are still green.

The figure floating above Africa now says five billion. I stare at the number, frowning.

'It can't be... you mean to say that Africa's population has quadrupled over the last sixty-five years?'

'Yes, exactly. Asia's not far behind either: They've nearly doubled in the same amount of time.'

'How could this happen? What about one-child policies?' I ask. 'If overpopulation is an issue, surely you'd have imposed them everywhere by now?'

He bursts out laughing.

'Don't be ridiculous. You can't impose a one-child policy in democracies, it's impossible. People just won't do it unless they're forced. And how would you enforce it? Any government that's tried has been toppled. Nobody has the guts to do what's necessary.' Groebler sniggers unpleasantly.

Burke chimes in, 'China was the only country to ever apply a one-child policy and that's how they developed into the number one economic power in the world. But as soon as they became a democracy, any attempt at population control collapsed.'

Groebler taps on Africa and it starts to throb, pulsating in a deep, dark red. 'Elsewhere – forget about imposing anything at all. I was born in Africa; believe me, things will never change there. These people just want to buy a goat and raise a family of ten. That's how they define success and happiness. We won't be able to convince them to stop multiplying.'

'If that's what they want, who are we to say otherwise?' Olivia says.

He shakes his head, irritated. 'What about the rest of us? They're putting the world in jeopardy and you feel sorry for them because they can't live out their dream?' The Colonel's voice rises now, as he becomes increasingly absorbed in what he's saying.

'When the United Nations started to become aware of the overpopulation crisis, they asked the international community to show self-control and produce fewer children – and guess who did it? We did. White snowflakes like you took pledges to have one child or none. And what did the rest of the world do? They just continued to proliferate and now we're overrun. That's why in the Coalition countries, we actually encourage fertility.'

'What?' Olivia says, all doe-eyed and guileless. 'But that's mad – if there isn't enough food for everyone anymore, why add to the issue?'

'Because the white race is being wiped out, fast. That's what's really happening. Maybe white women like you should stop being so fucking squeamish and spread your legs more often.'

Olivia goes beetroot red and looks at her shoes.

'We waited too long to work on a global solution. White populations are going to die because of self-restraint, while the rest of the world breeds their way into a catastrophic shit show.'

He looks at his iMode. 'Captain Burke, finish the assessment without me, I've seen enough. You're leaving for Uganda on Monday at zero six hundred hours. As you're in charge of the Kampala operations and stationed locally anyway, you'll oversee their mission there, as well. Make the necessary preparations. I expect reports every week and ongoing evaluations of their ability to continue.'

He turns and leaves the room, not even putting on the pretense of civility anymore.

I see the back of him with relief. As the door closes, Olivia and I look at each other.

'Can you believe how racist...' Olivia starts, but I stop her, shaking my head.

Burke lets out an embarrassed chuckle. 'Apologies, Colonel Groebler does get overworked when the topic is Africa. Please don't take it personally.' He looks at me. 'We're completely aware that you're American and we don't lump you in with the Africans.'

I'm even more appalled at this than I was by Groebler's straight-out racism, but I keep my face straight. So what does he mean? That he tolerates my skin color because I have the right passport?

'Why is Colonel Groebler so angry?' Olivia asks.

'You have to understand, he's an Afrikaner,' Burke says, as if it explained anything. Seeing our blank looks, he adds, 'When food started to become scarce, riots broke out all over the world. In 2071, things got particularly bad in South Africa. The government had done a piss-poor job of running the country but could hardly admit that the famine and unrest were their fault, so they looked for a scapegoat. There was still a large population of Afrikaners there and the government blamed them, saying they were parasites who had pilfered the country's resources and exploited the locals for too long. They massacred thousands of whites and the rest fled. Groebler's family was killed. He was on mission for the Programme and only learned about it when he came back. There was nothing he could have done, but he still blames himself.'

I don't believe this is the whole truth. Funny how white Africans keep pushing the narrative of being victims of genocide. I keep my face impassive and bite the inside of my cheek.

Olivia looks appalled. She asks for details and Burke says he had a wife and two young sons under ten years old.

'Afrikaners were stripped of their nationalities by the South African government and all their possessions were nationalized or appropriated. It happened all over Africa after that, like dominoes: Zimbabwe, Namibia, Sudan, Niger. Most African-born whites are now refugees in Europe or Australia, it's the new diaspora of this century.'

'I'm so sorry,' Captain Burke says, sitting down next to me. 'We don't all feel like him. He's just concerned about your safety and wants to make sure you come back to the KEW in one piece.' He smiles charmingly.

'The queue?' I ask.

'No, no, the Kingdom of England and Wales. Home.' His eyebrows crease and then rise. 'Oh that's right, you don't know about the triple secession yet.'

Olivia looks pensive. 'The flag... of course.' She says it more to herself than anyone else.

'Scotland and Ireland broke off after we left the United States of Europe.' He glances at his iMode bracelet. 'We're late. I need to take you to the shooting range to evaluate your skills with a gun.'

He gets up and we follow him through a maze of hallways and down to the building's basement. There, he watches as Olivia and I learn to assemble and disassemble the new models of guns. They're very similar to the old ones. But these ones have a DNA 'fingerprint' which means they can only be fired by the person who owns them.

While we handle the firearms, Burke carries on explaining. 'There were retaliations when we dared to leave the USE, Europeans were sore losers, but you know us – stiff upper lip, self-control and all that.' He smiles. 'We can withstand anything. So we just became an autarky of sorts. Now we produce pretty much everything we need and what we don't make ourselves we get from our allies, the US, Australia and Russia.'

'Why those three countries?' I ask.

'Because we're all part of the Coalition.'

'It must be hard to be completely closed off, not having access to foreign things. Don't you feel isolated sometimes?' Olivia asks.

'I've never known anything else. This happened before I was born.' He shrugs. 'And at least that way we took back control of our national destiny and our immigration policies.' I feel him glance at me and wonder what he really means by that. 'So it was all worth it.'

Ear protectors on, we spend a couple of hours acquainting ourselves with the guns as Burke shows us the new features. He helps Olivia with her stance, from behind, holding her arms up as he wraps himself around her. She lets him. Of course she does. It's like a revolting rom-com set in a neo-Nazi future.

He only looks at her as he speaks. I see her through his eyes: A perfect specimen of a white English rose. Her red hair and freckles, her milky white skin, her fertile hips and soft curves. Suddenly I feel too dark, too hard and dried up. Not the kind of woman anyone here would want. He takes Olivia's elbow solicitously and whispers that she should be particularly careful in Africa. She'll be a prime target but he'll be there to protect her. I feel nauseous.

Next, Burke drones on about the implications of the UK disbandment and the topic comes to the royal family. I hide an eye roll as he expands on the sorry status of his shrunken country and its useless monarchy. 'Scotland and Ireland are both republics now. The King's a bit of a womanizer and he hasn't married, so we've plenty of bastards but no heir.'

'What about the princess?'

'Nah, she's been removed from the line of succession, she married a black guy.' He shrugs.

Under cover of light banter, he's observing us. Observing how Olivia misses her target, how I know how to handle a gun but don't seem to hit the target either. The man is subtle, perceptive and definitely competent. I make a mental note of that and continue to fake my ineptitude.

At length, we make our way back upstairs. Now that I'm more aware of the political situation, I notice that there are very few people of color in the building and I start to feel completely out of place. Olivia and Burke walk ahead of me and as we round a corner, a middle-aged woman bumps into me and says under her breath, 'Go home, you dirty monkey.' I barely react and ignore it as I always do. It's not worth the trouble of responding. But the pang of hurt stabs my gut anyway.

Burke puts a hand on the small of Olivia's back and she looks up at him, listening attentively. Suddenly, I feel alone and the world seems vast and dark.

19

OLIVIA

*C*onurbation of London, November 2081

I WAKE up with a start and feel a hand over my mouth. Adrenaline kicks in and I try to take a breath to scream but my eyes adjust to the night and I realise that it's only Madison. The young woman holds her hand on my mouth until I nod, then she lets go and motions for me to follow her. It's half past midnight. Puzzled, I quickly put on my trainers and the jacket, wishing I had one of my comfy M&S cardigans to wrap up in instead.

I crawl out of my pod and quietly follow Madison outside the flat, closing the door behind me, as I shiver in the dark corridor.

'What is g—'

She brings a finger to her lips, shakes her head and starts to walk away.

I hesitate. Why didn't we wake up DeAnn? Where is she

taking me? What do I know about Madison, really? Should I leave behind the only person I know? My only partner?

Madison is ten steps ahead now. She stops and turns back to me, gesturing urgently. Curiosity wins over fear and I follow her through endless corridors. In the dark everything looks eerie and I'm cold. After a good five minutes we reach a lift, Madison waves her wrist and requests the second to last floor.

We ascend in silence. Under the service lift's neon lights, Madison looks tired and older than this morning; fine lines crisscross underneath her eyes and her mouth has a bitter slant. She's still completely silent, eyes averted, so I follow her example.

At length, the lift doors open with a ping, revealing a large deserted kitchen where the stainless steel counters and appliances glint dully in the darkness. Madison motions urgently and we climb the last floor using a service staircase. We arrive in a long and narrow service area where a slender woman is already standing motionless in the shadows near a trolley piled up with glasses and china. I hear male voices arguing on the other side of the wall and for a long while, we just stand there, eavesdropping on a conversation that means nothing to me. Whenever I glance at Madison, she places a finger against her lips. The other woman is wrapped in a cloak, her frail silhouette pressed against the wall. She must be peering through a spyhole.

Time passes.

Then, as I'm starting to sway from exhaustion, my ears prick up at the mention of my name.

'The Sagewright girl is malleable... I ... 2016 evaluations ... no business being a field agent.' The voice has a clipped South African cadence and the man sounds derisive. Groebler.

There seem to be five or six people in the room next to ours and we can't hear everything they say through the wall. But I'm sure I heard my name. I frown and Madison raises her eyebrows, shaking her head in alarm.

'What about the other one? The nigger.' A low voice, an American man.

'She seems harmless.' Groebler answers again. 'The 2016 files ranked her well... lower standard... do today... poorly against my man earlier.'

'We should just secure the... It's too risky.' An Australian accent, deep voice, muffled, through the wall.

'Colonel, do you think... can be contained?' De Courcy's voice.

'Absolutely. They're amateurs. They should never have become field agents... can keep them under control for a year.'

'Let's hope we won't have to wait a whole year...'

'I really think my men would be the best choice, it's easier and they're...'

Sounds of protest rise and arguments break out.

'Under no circumstances. The fact that they're on your territory now doesn't mean you have the right to...'

'I'll have to report this to my superiors, do you hear me?'

'No, no, that's not what I'm saying at all. But it's a big risk to take, just because we can't agree. It'd be easier to simply extract... keep... safe...'

It sounds like de Courcy's trying to placate them and restore order. 'OK, OK, fine. We'll... All in favour?'

Silence. I assume they're raising hands. Muffled grumbling.

Madison and the slender woman start towards the exit and I follow them, but as I walk past, I bump into the trolley. The glasses vibrate tentatively against each other; I freeze, holding my breath until the tinkling stops. Feeling like an idiot for nearly toppling it, I blush under their glares. When the sound subsides, they tiptoe away and I hurry after them. We take the stairs quietly and the two women only stop when we're back in the kitchen, one floor below.

'What was that all about?'

'Keep your voice down, Olivia, you never know who might be listening in this building.' Madison looks grave.

'What on earth is going on? Will you answer me?'

The woman removes her hood, revealing white hair that gleams in the moonlight. She's in her nineties or maybe older, frail and very thin. Her pale, wrinkled face breaks into a smile. 'Olivia, it's good to see you again.'

'What are you talking about? I've never met you before in my life.'

'It's not important. There isn't much time. I need to explain a few things.'

'You can start by telling me who you are.'

Madison opens her mouth to protest at my tone but the frail old woman holds up a hand.

'It's alright.' She turns her penetrating eyes to me. 'We are the last members of the Cassandra Resistance. We don't mean you any harm. I knew your father, you see.'

How can that be? That means she must be at least one hundred years old. I'm busy doing the maths when she continues.

'We worked on the Cassandra Programme together at its inception. He was a wonderful man. I owe him a lot.'

'OK, that's nice but what does it have to do—'

'Just listen, there's no time. If I'm caught here, I'll be executed on sight. You're in grave danger. The Cassandra Programme was taken over by the Helenus, the year you left. They're working with the Coalition now.'

I start to ask a question but she holds her hand up, looking over her shoulder towards a noise in the darkness. We wait a few minutes, holding our breath, then she relaxes and continues.

'They need your microchips in order to go back to 2016 and change the future in their favour. This cannot be allowed to happen.'

'But what do you mean they need our chips? What about us?'

'They'll kill you of course, and send back two Helenus agents in your place.'

Oh shit.

'We were lucky tonight, their internal divisions played in our favour; they can't agree yet on who should go back once you're dead. The Helenus is struggling to maintain control over the Programme, while the governments who sponsor the operations want to take over, militarily if need be.

Meanwhile, none of the Coalition countries trusts the others enough to select two agents to represent all of their interests. They each want the technology for themselves. So they've bought themselves a year to decide and while they squabble, you live. But you'll be under the Programme's close surveillance at all times, that of Groebler's men particularly.'

The ground drops under my feet. 'But what do you mean? Are you saying that I only have a year left to live?'

Madison and the old woman exchange a glance.

'Well, yes,' the young woman says. 'Unless they can reach their decision on whom to send in your place before the year is up, then you'd have less than a year.'

'What? But, but...' My chest feels tight and I can't breathe. Taking long gulps of air, I start to feel dizzy and have to sit down on the kitchen floor. 'But none of this makes any bloody sense! We're in a bloody Programme facility. Why don't they use their own bloody microchips to go back to 2016? What do they bloody want with mine?'

Madison and the old woman frown and glance at each other, then the old woman's face clears.

'But of course, I forgot. You're not...' she stops. 'Don't you remember from your *agent* training, Olivia?' She crouches in front of me and glances pointedly at Madison, so only I'll see it. 'Calm down and think. You know that the technology only allows forward travel. We can only ever go to the future, Olivia, remember?'

I nod as my stomach drops even further. Am I stuck here, then? But de Courcy said we could go back. My head is spinning.

Madison throws uncertain glances at me, over her shoulder, as she keeps watch over the deserted kitchen. The old woman helps me up, her wrinkled face very close to my ear, she whispers, 'Microchips are like boomerangs. They only go back to the year they started out from. The only way for the Coalition to go back in time and change the past is to steal yours.'

Back on my feet, I drink a few mouthfuls of air and try to compose myself. 'Who are these guys anyway?'

'De Courcy and Groebler works for the Helenus and the rest of them are representing each one of the Coalition's governments,' Madison says, frowning at me. 'We no longer run the Programme, they do. For corporate profit and for the benefit of their governments' twisted ideology.' She continues, 'So if they go back instead of you, they'll change the last sixty-five years, hunt us down, eradicate the people who don't fit with their—'

The old woman holds up a hand. 'Not if we can prevent it. Olivia will not let us down.'

Madison looks at me dubiously.

Shit, shit, shit. This is not good. I am not qualified to do this. I take a shaky breath.

'OK, what do I do?'

The old woman has been watching my face closely and after a moment of silence she says pensively, 'The purity of your genetic heritage will appeal to them and your symbolic value as the Sagewright daughter will be a prize, a rallying banner, giving legitimacy to whoever claims you. Even if they take your chip, there's a chance they might spare you and let you live in this timeline. The Resistance could still use you, if you can infiltrate their ranks.'

I splutter, 'I beg your pardon?'

'Please pay attention, Olivia, I have to go soon. I want you to pretend to agree with the Coalition's views. Pretend that you'd be interested in staying, in having an affair with one or several of them. Convince them that you'd consider donating your chip to a man, better qualified than you for the return mission. But covertly, I want you to gather as much information as you can on them. Send me actionable intel: their names, their faces, their plans, their weapons, all of it.'

I'm feeling cold. All of this is starting to be a bit much. I shiver and wrap my arms around myself. The darkness presses against my chest as I rub the scab on my forearm, feeling the microchip move just under my skin. I want to go home.

Madison strokes her pregnant belly as a flicker of doubt passes across her features but the old woman's face softens and she puts a hand on my arm.

'I'm counting on you being your father's daughter, Olivia. You can do it. You have to do it. Your life depends on it. All our lives depend on it.'

That's brilliant, no pressure at all then.

'What about DeAnn?'

'You cannot tell her anything.'

'Why not?'

'This has happened before. Olivia... I... I cannot say more. Just don't involve her.'

'How could this have happened already? I'm so confused.'

'It's complicated, there's no time to explain. I jumped forward, I have read the report about your mission. You... Just trust me, Olivia, and don't tell DeAnn.'

I scoff. 'Trust you? I don't even know you.'

'And you think you know her? Do you think she'd hesitate to sacrifice you to save herself? There is no way to know what she might do. We can't afford to trust her and have you both killed before you can gather the intel the Resistance needs. You can't tell her anything.'

'But what will I do, on my own, if they try to murder me? You heard them, I'm not cut out for this – she can help.'

'This is not up for discussion, Agent Sagewright. You will work for us and leave DeAnn out of it, or we will take the appropriate measures to terminate your mission and make sure the Resistance prevails. Understood?'

A clanging noise interrupts us.

A man's voice rings out. 'Who's there? Identify yourself.'

We drop to a crouch under the nearby steel-top table and stay very still. Gumshoes squeak on the tiled floor and a torch beam shines as it moves around the room, looking for us.

Madison is struggling, her balance impaired by her bump. She sways and starts to fall but I catch her. Holding our breath, our eyes fixed on the shadows, we strain to hear what the guard is doing. Bending low, the three of us hurry out of the office, while the man checks the far side of the room. We slink out and run to the staircase.

The older woman exchanges a quick hug with Madison, then she squeezes my shoulder and disappears down the stairwell, her cloak billowing behind her in the dark.

Madison and I dash back through the corridors to the normal lift and step into it. As we catch our breaths, she starts an innocuous conversation with me about the midnight snacks one can get on rations. I look at her blankly so she moves her eyes up. I follow her gaze to a camera. She continues talking happily about her favourite biscuits. I play along, thanking her for helping me find some food at this late hour. We part when we reach my floor. She presses my hand warmly in both of hers, her expression grave. The lift doors close and I find myself alone in the deserted hallway. It seems darker and colder than before, as I walk back to bed alone, jumping at every sound.

Rattled, I toss and turn in my coffin bed, unable to go to sleep. How can I not tell DeAnn? She's the only person I actually know here.

On the other hand, she denounced me when we were in training and thinks I'm an idiot. She's been cold towards me since the beginning and she said quite clearly that she tried to have me expelled.

But what do I know about the mystery woman? She knew my father, so what? Anyone could lie about that and even if it's true, it doesn't mean anything; he might not have liked her. Come to think of it, I'm not at all sure about her either. What did she mean 'terminate my mission'? Would she kill me too, if I failed to help the Resistance? I chew on my lower lip, as fear tugs at my guts. I didn't even think to ask her name. I'm an idiot. I'm in way over my head. What the heck have I gotten mixed up in?

20

DEANN

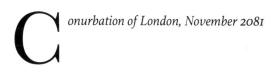

onurbation of London, November 2081

THE NEXT DAY, Olivia and I are allowed off-duty time to do a few last things in London before our departure for Uganda.

The smartest thing to do would be to leave right now and chance it out there for a year, on my own. But it's not very likely, is it? Colonel Groebler and de Courcy won't just let me wander off. Even if I could escape them, the iMode has scanned my DNA and everywhere I went, they'd be able to trace me. I can't really function in this future without an iMode, without money and without any type of network. And there's the small issue of access to a pyramid. How will I make my way back to 2016 without access to the Programme's facilities?

I sigh and shake my head. It looks like I'm going to have to play ball for a while longer. Every instinct in my body is shouting that this is a bad idea. But I can't see any way around it.

Frustrated by the lack of information and the powerlessness I'm feeling, I decide to do something simple and comforting: fix the catastrophe that is my hair.

It's a trek to get to the only black hairdresser's I've been able to find for miles around, and when I get nearer, I start having second thoughts about the whole thing. On the way into the neighborhood, two bored policemen in riot gear hardly spare me a glance when my iMode bracelet flashes blue as I cross through a metal gate blocking the street. Frowning, I make my way through the dilapidated neighborhood, noticing the drug addicts and homeless people, the once-white paint flaking off buildings in gray patches, the grimy sidewalks littered with fast food wrappings. There seem to be only people of color around.

I hesitate at the entrance of the busy hair salon, its cheerful yellow walls beckoning as Jamaican music blasts out, drowned by the joyful hubbub of conversations. Half a dozen clients are getting their hair done and one of the hairdressers is dancing, as the others laugh and clap, their colorful, patterned leggings and the wheeze of hairdryers blending with the overall activity and bustle in irresistible chaos.

'Come in, my love, come in, we don't bite!' A smiling, plump woman invites me in as her clients roar with laughter.

A few hours later, having soaked in the gossip and inconspicuously tried to gain some information, I emerge, my hair dyed black, straightened and trimmed, finally looking like myself again. Not as good as a weave but once straightened within an inch of its life, my own hair is reasonably shiny, a good surprise. But on my way out of the neighborhood, I have to wait in line for nearly half an hour and this time, the guards check my iMode, question me about my reason for leaving and frisk me.

At last they let me go and I'm once again in the city. Absorbed in gloomy thoughts, I make a wrong turn and find myself in a crowd outside an ugly concrete building. Reporters are making excited speeches in front of lit-up cameras. Intrigued, I stop and listen to one of the journalists' reports.

' ... about to come out of the Old Bailey Criminal Court where the case of Alvita and Amani Clarke is being decided today. The fourth-generation Caribbean couple was arrested last year for breaking the AEP law. Instead of accepting deportation...'

Someone presses against me in the crowd and when I turn to snap at them, I realize it's only an old black woman, her curly gray hair pulled into a neat bun, the strands of whiter hair shining in the morning sun. The old woman is pulling a green crocheted cardigan tightly against her thin frame, watching avidly, straining to hear what's happening. She reminds me of my grandmother.

I remember going to see my grandma in her nursing home, a week after Barack Obama won the election. She was the granddaughter of a house servant and had told me many stories about her childhood in the age of slavery. She was so proud of me, the doctor. Something told me I should come that day; I didn't do it often, maybe once a year.

I'd shown her the photos of President Obama and the press articles to prove that he'd been elected, and she'd looked at it all. Her frail, bony hands handled the photos, trembling as she unconsciously bit her dentures. She'd looked at me over her bifocal glasses.

'Oooh, DeAnn, it's you.'

She raised her shaky hand and touched my cheek and then went back to the photos with a frown, her head shaking back and forth, her voice quavering with age.

'So this young man, a negro...'

'We don't say that word anymore, Grandma.'

'A negro has been elected president?' She had a slight drawl and it sounded like 'pray-zee-dayn't'.

'Yes, Grandma, an African American in the White House,' I said, my heart swelling with hope and pride.

She shook her head, disbelieving, marveling, afraid to rejoice, and just kept saying, 'Well, I'll be. Well, well... Are you sure?'

Grandma died a month later and I kept the image of her wondering face like a precious treasure in my jewelry box.

Someone steps on my foot and I snap back to the London street. I place a gentle hand on the old woman's arm and she jumps, startled, then looks at me in alarm but her face relaxes when she sees that I'm black too.

'You shouldn't be here. It's dangerous,' she says, taking in my clothes and my hair.

Puzzled, I wonder why and ask, 'What about you?'

'I had to come. I had to see it.' She tightens her green cardigan around her.

To me, it looks like an ordinary scene: A mildly hyped civil case of some sort. Journalists love to add this kind of social sob stories at the end of the news segment. Makes them look like they give a shit.

'See what?' I ask.

'History,' she whispers. 'They hope we'll die out. But we won't. No, we won't.' She points to the court's entrance with her chin. 'Some of us choose to fight.' She crosses her arms, hugging herself, her jaw working, lips pressed.

The journalist presses a finger against his ear and looks

away from the camera, turning his head toward where a couple have emerged, journalists pressing them on all sides. The dark-skinned woman looks intensely uncomfortable as she hides her small son behind her and places a protective hand on her pregnant belly.

'Janet, there's movement, it looks like we're going to have a statement any minute now,' the journalist says.

The family stops and huddles together, unable to go any further. A barrister, wearing a ridiculous robe and wig, steps in front of them and pulls out his iMode, then starts to read from it – the verdict concerning his clients, I'm guessing. I'm too far to hear but the crowd doesn't seem very pleased with the results.

The journalist turns back to the camera, visibly surprised. 'Well, Janet, it's an unprecedented verdict here today at the Old Bailey. The court is releasing the Clarkes. It appears that the family will not receive a jail sentence, fines or sanctions of any kind despite the fact that...'

He presses his finger to his ear and goes silent for a few seconds. 'The family is not being deported, Janet, they'll stay in the KEW. Well, this is completely unexpected. We can expect an appeal against the judge's decision, which is – to say the least – astonishing. A non-white family allowed to reproduce, this is unacceptable and I...'

The crowd is becoming violent; a group of beefy young white men is hurling invectives at the couple and some of the people of color in the crowd interpose themselves. A fight breaks out and I try to extricate myself from the milling mass. I plant my feet down but the crowd surges, pulling me forward toward the thugs who are starting to punch the Clarkes. The father is bleeding from his nose, his arms open to protect his child, who is cowering behind him. I hear the mother's screams from somewhere on the ground; I can only see the hateful, contorted faces of the men who are kicking her in the stomach. The police are nowhere to be seen.

There's not much I can do for them, so I take the old woman by the arm and steer us toward the street I came from. A well-dressed elderly man leaning on a walking stick spots us. His face scrunches up in resolution, he marches toward us and I think he's going to offer us help but instead he raises his cane and as I lunge to protect the old woman, his cane strikes my forehead. My reflexes kick in and I push him violently so that he falls backward. I step over him and pull the old lady with me. We run to the Tube station.

'Are you OK?' I say when we reach the top of the staircase, both of us shaking and winded.

Her head is shaking and her jaw is working, soundlessly.

'History,' she says, as a wan smile stretches across her lips.

I try to check her vitals but she just pats my hand and leaves, hurrying down the steps silently. As her frail silhouette is swallowed by darkness, I wipe an angry tear off my cheek.

21

OLIVIA

onurbation of London, November 2081

I STARE at the council estate and the drab street in front of me. This is where the cottage should be, but I don't recognise anything. On the iBubble screen, a map is superimposed over the landscape, but I just can't match the address to where I'm standing. I collapse the glass sphere and massage my temples, trying to get rid of the headache that's been building up since this morning. It must be somewhere around here. I'm probably lost. Typical.

Home.

In my mind's eye, I imagine Mum's house, my favourite spot on earth. Some places have magic in them. Wisteria, honeysuckle and clematis grow against the red brick walls and tickle the slanted roof. A barrel sits at a corner to collect rainwater.

The air smells of mowed grass and the sun timidly

warms my hand on the garden gate latch. The rugged wood feels familiar under my palm. I stop to drink in the sight of this house that makes me feel grounded and happy, and then continue my morning tour of the garden, relishing the feel of the grass under my feet, the wet kiss of the morning dew on my ankles.

'Oh, how wonderful, you're awake, sunshine.'

A tear rolls down my cheek as I press my eyes shut against the dreariness of 2081. Instead of opening my eyes, I imagine Mum tightening her terrycloth robe, her face still full of sleep. She meets me halfway, stopping here and there to pick up a few dead leaves and a rose. I hug her as she wraps me in a warm embrace. We stay like that for a little while, hugging each other and smiling.

She touches my red hair. 'You're so beautiful in the morning.'

The smell of wood wax and the empty silence greet us as I close the front door behind us, holding the cold milk bottle in my hand.

I remember when this house was full of sound and bois-terous life. My brother charging down the stairs two by two, clamouring for his breakfast. Our chocolate lab, Jasper, barking and dropping the ball at Dad's feet, asking him to play. Mum calling, 'Breakfast's ready!' in a loud clear voice, and me, curled up on the window sill with a book, Tolkien or some other fantasy novel, looking up from my dream world to find my brother ready to pounce and tickle me until I cried for mercy.

Everything is exactly as always; the small Sheraton desk at the entrance where books are piled up haphazardly, the muddy Wellington boots in a row under the coats, the old copper coal bucket ending its days by the entrance as an umbrella stand.

She's re-upholstered the sofa again, I notice, amused. The colour doesn't quite match the rest of the room. She's always fiddling with the front room. But it's never quite right. There's a large bouquet of white lilies on the mantel of the black cast iron fireplace. Their smell overpowers this room as it always does. The vase of lilies is always there. As soon as they wilt, she buys more. Always white ones. I never thought to ask why. I should.

The ghost smell of the lilies tickles my nose. I adjust my iBubble and will myself back into the daydream.

Mum's in the kitchen, humming as she toasts the crumpets. For a minute, I look at her hunched shoulders, choked up. She's only seventy-one but I'm starting to notice how fast she gets tired, the new lines on her face, the liver spots on her hands. What will I do without her?

I remember when the house smelled of burnt apricot jam, and my dad and my brother would come back from their walks, their tempers high.

'Why can't you be more sensible? I'll stop supporting you if you drop out of—' my father would begin.

'I don't care,' my brother would interrupt. 'You always do this, always force me to be like you.' Dermot was always so stubborn.

'I'm doing no such thing, I'm just trying to do what's best for you, but you're so headstrong, you only ever do what you want.'

'Of course I do. This is my life, not yours. You don't care who I really am.'

'How will you feed yourself? You can't rely on me all your life.'

'Rely on you? You're never even here!'

They never quite saw eye to eye and little by little the

house became more tense and subdued between fights, more explosive when they locked horns.

Then my brother died. Then my father.

Now the house is silent and it smells of lilies. My mother is growing old here, alone. Who will learn the pudding recipes? Who will inherit this cottage? Who will remember these ghosts when I'm gone?

The familiar anxiety tugs at my belly, reminding me that the survival of my family is my responsibility and that I'm failing in my duty. I'm the last link in a long chain of people that has existed for centuries. And this chain will break because I'm incapable of finding someone to love me enough to perpetuate my genetic patrimony. I'm an evolutionary dead end. The weak link. Or rather the broken link, the last link. Tears sting my eyes and I swallow them back.

'Mum?'

'Yes, sunshine,' she says as the bread springs out of the toaster.

The green cupboards happily echo the green of spring outside the window. The kettle is on and Mum's in her bathrobe. I've been afraid of her reaction about the IVF. Such a messy unconventional way towards motherhood, I'm afraid she'll disapprove.

When I tell her, instead of criticising, she hugs me fiercely and a few buttons of her nightgown come open, her heavy breasts visible, drooping; I avert my eyes but she catches my hand.

'Sunshine, you have to become a mother. It's what will make you a woman. You can't consider yourself fully grown until you've given birth.' She grabs me and presses both our hands against her belly.

I'm completely taken by surprise, repulsed by how physical she is. She's so profoundly anchored in her own body. Her fleshy rolls of skins are warm under my hand.

'Motherhood comes from the gut,' she says in a low intense whisper.

I yank my hand back and wish she'd close her night-dress, but she's too absorbed in passing me this all-important message, that she hasn't even realised it's gaping open. Her breasts sway a little, pointing downward.

'Mum, the IVF actually has a very low percentage of success at my age and...'

'You will make me a baby.'

'What? No, I'm not making a baby for you or with you. Why would you put it like that?'

She turns to me, sunlight playing with the curls on her neck and then she vanishes, as this grey, suffocating day in 2081 erases all trace of her.

I Know It doesn't matter and there are more pressing concerns. Like the small fact that I'm not an agent and I'm in over my head. Or the fact that the Programme was attacked before we left and they might not have time to rebuild the pyramid before we make it back. Or the fact that the Coalition is out to kill us. And I know it's stupid and I know that it's not technically my home anymore as I'm probably dead by now, but I'd still like to find it. I wipe my palms against my leggings and sigh.

Oh wait – first, I need to check that I'm really dead; I wouldn't want to run into myself and ruin the universe's balance or something like that. I check my iMode and here it is, in my Programme personnel file: deceased.

'Well, that's not creepy at all, is it?' I say to no one in

particular. So, how did I die? And when...? Oh, God. The temptation to open up the file is nearly more than I can resist. I really shouldn't know, I'll spend the rest of my life obsessing over it and then counting down to the moment. But what if I can prevent it? What if I need to know this? In the end, fear wins. I just don't want to know.

I spot a group of old men drinking beer, standing outside one of the towers' entrances. Not great, but I guess they'll have to do. We start chatting and then they break my heart.

'I know the one you mean: a small cottage with a big field around it, innit?'

'Yes, that's right. It should be close by, do you know where I can find it?'

He snorts with laughter. Actually snorts. 'You're standing on it, love.'

'What?'

'They built the council estate on it. Couldn't just carry on belonging to one person, not with all the honest folk needing housing and what have you.'

'But how could this happen? Didn't it belong to someone?'

'Yeah, I remember, there was a woman who lived there alone. She died and no one inherited the house, so it went to the council and they razed it.'

I wonder if he's talking about my mum or me. The woman lived alone. She died alone. She had no one to pass her home down to. A shudder snakes up my spine; maybe I'm standing on my own grave. My worst fears realised. I died alone and failed my family.

'Motherhood comes from the gut' I hear, like an echo through time.

22

DEANN

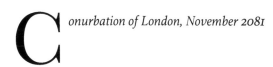

onurbation of London, November 2081

'WELCOME.' Madison is on the threshold, smiling, a toddler balanced on her hip as Olivia, Burke and I get out of the driverless cab.

We cram into the minuscule hallway and Madison's husband, Darren, announces through the kitchen door, 'Dinner's nearly ready.'

We hear a few pots clanging and cooking smells waft over. I wonder if this time it'll be edible. Anthony disappears into the kitchen, ostensibly to help Darren, more likely to have a beer with him.

'Mummy, Mummy, Mummy!'

A little girl of about four sprints toward us, but she skids to a halt when she sees me. Hiding behind her mother's legs, she looks up at us with huge blue eyes, her gaping mouth displaying decayed and missing teeth.

I get the sense that inviting people to one's home has become an event in this society. Of course if there's a food shortage, everyone would want to keep the food for their own family, not share it.

'Hello, Jenny.' Olivia crouches in front of the child but the little girl ignores her and stares at me, eyes wide. She reaches over tentatively and touches my knee, then squeals and runs to the kitchen, swivelling her head every other step to check that we're still here.

Madison takes our jackets and whispers, 'Please be cautious, they don't know anything, of course.'

We both nod and follow her to the living room.

There's a bit of a commotion in the kitchen and as I pass the open door, I hear a whispered conversation.

'Mummy's friend is brown, Daddy, I touched her skin but it doesn't come off.'

'Wash your hands, right now, Jenny.'

And I thought nothing could get to me anymore.

This is one of the smallest living rooms I've ever seen, littered with toys and with threadbare furniture. A table is laid in the middle, taking up all the space, the seven plates jostling with each other to fit on it. The chairs are a mish-mash of styles and there are fake flowers in a vase in the middle.

Madison sets the little boy on the sofa. She snaps the bracelet off her wrist, flattens it and pulls on its corners in a practiced gesture, as she chats to us. The clear plastic stretches like moulding clay until it reaches the size of a small tablet, then she gives the kid the extended iMode. On the transparent screen, I get a glimpse of Paddington's familiar silhouette.

'Mummy, go see real bear?'

'No, sweetheart, we can't. They're all gone.'

'Where bears go, Mummy? When come back?'

She kisses the top of her little boy's head. 'They're all in heaven, sweetheart. They're not coming back.'

Olivia's face contracts with pity and sadness but Madison doesn't seem to realize the magnitude of what her children have lost. I guess she never saw a bear either. I go wash my hands and when I come back, Madison and Olivia are in the garden, having what looks like a pretty intense conversation.

Foregoing discretion, I decide I want to know what they're saying and carefully open the french windows to the garden, edging closer to the handkerchief-sized vegetable plot at the back.

'You have to promise to save my family. When you go back.' Madison sounds distressed. 'I will help you, I swear... but only if my children...' Her voice breaks. 'You have to promise you'll make sure they're born.'

I try to get closer and miss a part of the whispered conversation: '...a number to call,' I hear Madison say.

'Is it the woman we met yesterday?' Olivia asks.

What the hell is going on?

'Shh...' She unclasps Olivia's iMode and dictates a phone number to it but just as she starts to say the name 'A —', I make a noise and they both flinch and fall silent.

'I was just walking Olivia through my vegetable garden and showing her how to take a photo of it on her iMode.' Madison gives an embarrassed little chuckle.

She returns Olivia's iMode and pretends to give us a tour of the minuscule gardening plot, and I let her rattle on as I try to work through what I just heard. The day is overcast but warm and muggy and the summery temperature throws me off. I keep forgetting we're in November, it's at least 68°F. Something else is nagging me but I can't really put my finger on it. Then it hits me: the garden is completely silent.

There are no flying, buzzing insects, no birds chirping, no sound of barking dogs in the neighborhood. Nothing. Frowning, I get back to the conversation.

'Do you grow any fruits?' I ask.

'No, of course not, that's impossible,' Madison says, distracted.

'Is it because we're in November?'

Madison throws a glance inside, checking on her son; no one else is back in the living room yet. 'Sorry? Oh no, no, it's because the bees died.'

'What, all the bees?'

'Pretty much.'

'That's... wow.' Olivia's eyebrows rise.

'What happened?' I ask, somewhat more eloquently.

'Climate change? Pesticides? Who knows? They were such a fragile species, it was bound to happen sooner or later, I guess.' Madison shrugs. 'Anyway, here we all are: all bees are extinct and pretty much all fruits and vegetables have disappeared.'

'What?'

'Yes, no more pollination means no more apples, tomatoes, oranges – well, the list is so long, let's just say we're out of vegetables and fruits. We don't have things like cotton anymore either, or cocoa, coffee and vanilla...'

'You mean no more chocolate!' Olivia exclaims, while I think about a world without wine.

Madison seems distracted. She leads us back to the living room and tousles her son's blonde hair as she sits on the sofa. Just as Olivia and I settle down next to her, a TV turns itself on of its own accord with the words 'Breaking News' pulsating against a red backdrop. The screen is enormous and takes up pretty much the whole wall; actually, it looks like the wall *is* a TV.

The sound of machine guns erupts in the living room, scenes of blood splattered over walls, people being shot as they try to run away. The images are disturbingly clear and close-up.

The news commentator intones, 'A group of Alphas opened fire in an immigration center in Schistou, Greece just a few minutes ago. The attack is still under way, as you can see. There are forty-five casualties so far and one hundred and twenty-three injured. We're flying our reporter to the scene and will know more soon. At the moment, from the live surveillance footage, it looks like the attackers may have holed up in the East wing of the center.'

The sound subsides and I look away, nauseated. The boy is completely unfazed and goes back to the story he was reading, as if nothing had happened.

Madison says 'iMode, mute,' and the carnage continues in silence.

'What happened?' Darren calls from the kitchen.

'Nothing sweetheart, just migrants killed by Alphas.'

'Oh, OK,' he shouts back and we hear the sounds of cooking resume.

'What do you mean, "nothing"?' Olivia asks.

'Is this normal?' I ask, appalled.

'Well, it happens regularly, if that's what you mean.'

Before I have time to think of a question, Madison looks behind me with a smile for her husband. There's a confident sway in his step as he brings us drinks. Burke comes back as well, sits down on the carpet and starts playing with the boy.

We each take a glass of the bright blue drink. I hesitate to drink it, sneaking a glance at Darren, then take a tentative sip of the cocktail. Something chemical but strong. Olivia half chokes on hers as I relish the warmth spreading through my throat.

Darren sits next to Madison and kisses the side of her neck. 'I hope you haven't been boring them silly with politics, hon.'

Madison looks smitten with him. 'No, no, I was just showing them the gard—' Madison trills but I interrupt, annoyed by the fake pleasantries. I'm not here for the fucking canapés. I need to understand this time as soon as possible.

'So what just happened in Greece? Which terrorist group did this?'

'Oh, they're not terrorists, they're just Alphas.' Darren dismisses it with a wave of a hand. 'These things happen, boys will be boys.'

'It's not only boys anymore sweetheart, but yes they're just kids,' Madison adds, 'they go to immigration and refugee camps and kill as many applicants as they can to prevent them from getting into the USE.'

My shock is reflected on Olivia's face, but the others' absence of surprise betrays the number of times this has happened.

'You know how it is,' Burke says. 'Young hot heads get their hands on guns and take action.'

'What do you mean, take action? They just killed forty-five people. That doesn't sound like action to me, it sounds like mass murder.'

'Well, they have little say over the immigration policy of their bureaucracy over in Europe, so who could blame them for taking matters into their own hands? It's understandable. But they hardly kill any white people, so...' Darren stops mid-shrug, probably realizing that he's talking to me.

'So... what, Darren? So it doesn't matter as much, is that what you mean?'

Darren has the good grace to look uncomfortable. Madison is staring out the window at the garden plunged in darkness, running her fingers through the blond curls of her son, lost in her own thoughts.

'So Darren, what have you cooked? It smells delicious,' Olivia says.

Ignoring her awkward attempt to lighten the mood, I press on: 'Is immigration a big problem here?'

'Not here. But on the Continent, yes, they have several thousands arriving from Africa and the Middle East by boat practically every day,' Burke says. 'It's a huge security risk and a drain on their economy.' He shakes his head. 'Even with the best will in the world, Europe can't continue letting them all in. It's impossible, there are billions of them.'

'That's not the main issue,' Darren says, leaning back, both arms spreading on the sofa as he crosses his legs. 'The main problem is that the invasion has artificially inflated the Continent's fertility rates.'

'Wouldn't immigrants' fertility naturally lower after a generation or so in developed countries?' I ask, trying to get more information and pushing down my anger, for now.

'You might think so, but no, it didn't. They continued to have consistently higher fertility rates than white Europeans,' Burke answers, it takes at least two generations for their birth rates to lower to the host country's level.

Darren adds unpleasantly, 'And now, not only are they proliferating among themselves but they're also mixing with the general population. Whites made up about sixty percent of the population in Europe back in the noughties, but now with mixed marriages, there are fewer than twenty percent of pure whites on the Continent.' Darren shakes his head, disgusted.

'You always exaggerate, sweetheart. Anyway, shall we eat?' Madison interjects.

Throwing a glance at his wife, Darren presses his lips together and says, 'What we have has taken generations to build, we need to protect our way of life and our values. Our genetic heritage isn't just something we can lightly throw away.'

'Immigrants aren't polluting your bloodlines, they're enriching them,' I say, unable to keep quiet.

Darren snorts. 'When we visit Europe nowadays, it doesn't feel much like Europe anymore, does it? Everybody's brown. No offense, Diana.'

Olivia winces and throws a worried glance at me. 'As long as the culture is preserved, does it matter what color skin people are?' she says.

'Of course it does!' Darren blurts, getting heated. 'The culture is changing as well. It's influenced by what each migrant population brings with it. Can you believe that couscous, a North African dish, is now considered French cuisine? Or that Turkish words are in the German dictionary?'

'You make it sound like it's a bad thing. Evolution is good,' I say, stubbornly. 'Each minority enriches the host country with their diversity. Europe's sclerosis is obvious to me. Your countries *should* change and embrace the immigrants' cultures, not try to erase immigrants' backgrounds and assimilate them.'

'Oh yeah? Should we let them impose their religions and their backwardness too? Criminality has soared on the Continent. The immigrants have no idea what it's like to behave in our advanced society. They veil their women and rape ours simply because they wear normal clothes. The rates of theft, murder and interracial confrontations have skyrocketed in the USE. More and more folks are adhering to parties similar to the one in power here. We have networks of people helping us to spread the message in occupied Europe. Resist. Come to England. We can rebuild our civilization from here.'

Madison chuckles. 'Oh sweetie, you're so dramatic. You make it sound like the Continent is overrun by savages. It's hardly the case. They're doing just fine. They've chosen a different path to us, that's all.'

'Well, we're safe here. To curb the fertility issue, we deported all foreigners. They had no right to be here and were just stealing our benefits and polluting our way of life anyway.'

His wife tries to calm things down. 'We're an island, hon; we had the option to keep immigrants out, but the USE is an open continent; you know they had to make the best of it and open their borders to immigration. What else were they going to do, build a wall?' she adds jokingly.

'At least we're preserving our culture and only admitting immigrants from white countries.' Darren finishes his drink, looking annoyed.

'Thank God they did or we never would have met,' Madison laughs uncomfortably. 'He's Irish, you see, and I'm Canadian.' She turns to us. 'The main attraction about coming to England for white foreigners is that the KEW allows you to have as many children as you want, as long as you're white.'

The small living room is crackling with tension.

'Darling,' Madison says, patting Darren's knee and looking pointedly in the direction of the children, 'shall we get dinner started? It's getting late for the children.'

They're playing on the carpet, oblivious. Suddenly they both seem awfully white, with their blond curls and blue eyes.

The rest of the evening passes in lackluster conversation and uneasy small talk.

23

OLIVIA

*C*onurbation of London, November 2081

THE NEXT MORNING, I wake up and hit my head against the top of my coffin bed. Rubbing the bump, I lie back down and open the porthole as DeAnn comes out of the shower, naked. Of course, her body is completely hairless and perfect. Her midriff is flat as a board and her buttocks are tight and high. She gets dressed, unaware of the stab she's just inflicted to my self-confidence.

I open my mouth and close it again, hesitating to tell her about the Cassandra Resistance, but I couldn't do it here anyway, so I say nothing.

I bought some supplies during our downtime yesterday, so at least this morning we have shampoo and makeup, and I've ordered myself extra clothes and a pair of trousers that don't make me look like an overstuffed sausage.

We're ready to go at 5.30 a.m. Colonel Groebler picks us

up and Anthony whistles as he takes my bag and opens the van door for me. 'Wow, Olivia, you look nice.'

'Thank you, Anthony.' I giggle and blush as I climb into the van with them. Well, I might as well get started acting like the airhead idiot they think I am. It comes rather naturally, as he's buff and handsome, just my type, really. It was so cute the way he played with the boy yesterday and kept his calm while Darren and DeAnn were at each other's throats. He seems quiet and moderate. I play the part and shelve my thoughts for later.

DeAnn looks at us, her lips pressed together, frowning.

A few hours later, we finally make it through all the security and controls and board our plane. We find our seats and, feeling flustered and relieved, I turn on the air con. The dial is sticky and the seat has large, dark stains; rubbish is strewn on the floor.

Two passengers are sitting across the alley, chatting about doing business in Africa.

'Yeah, I sell furniture there. It's alright, I guess. Pays the bills.' The man has a Dutch accent.

Sitting on my left, a woman is dictating something into her iMode, it sounds like she's preparing a report for an NGO or something. She completely ignores me, holding a finger pressed on her iMode collar as she continues her whispered dictation.

There's a commotion at the front and a handful of policemen wearing bright yellow vests come into view, walking up the alley towards us. They're escorting a dozen Africans, leading them to the back of the plane. The prisoners' hands are bound, even those of the three young children among them. Someone bumps into me.

'Sorry, miss, I didn't see you there.' The English policeman who knocked my elbow off the armrest stops to apologise to me with a really nice smile. Then he roughly pulls the woman and her children by their handcuffs. They sit down and the policemen stand around the group of prisoners, blocking visibility and preventing access. A man starts screaming somewhere in the rear rows.

'I don't want to go back, don't make me, you can't make me go back, Aaaaaah! Stop breaking my arm! Somebody help me! I don't want to go back, don't make me, you can't make me go back, Aaaaaah! Stop breaking my arm! Somebody help me!' he screams in a loop at the top of his lungs.

Alarmed, I look for a stewardess to ask what's going on.

DeAnn gets up to help.

'Sit down. Now!' Groebler orders her between gritted teeth.

'But this is unacceptable!' she says. 'What the hell is going on?'

'Nothing, they're deportees. They're escorting them back to their countries,' Anthony says apologetically.

'But they're hurting them.' I get up as well.

The Dutch man shifts in his seat and whispers viciously, 'Sit down. Protesting is illegal, you should get arrested for what you're doing right now. Just let the police do their job.'

The Australian next to him chimes in, 'Well, it's the law and it's not a fun job but someone's got to do it.'

Two policemen come over. 'ID and ticket,' one of them asks DeAnn gruffly.

DeAnn looks like she wants to give him a piece of her mind but Burke lays a hand on her arm.

'It's alright, she's with me, officer.' Burke flips a badge open.

'Well, if she doesn't sit, I'll arrest her.'

Groebler smiles nastily, but lets Anthony sort it out with

the policeman. The other officer who jostled me earlier, smiles at me.

'Miss, you need to sit down too please.'

'But what are you doing to these people? Is the man really being hurt?'

He laughs. 'No, of course not. He was behaving completely normally when we were escorting him to the airport. He's just trying to attract people's attention now.'

I crane my neck towards the screaming man but it's impossible to see what they're doing to him, as he's being held down by half a dozen policemen.

I hesitate, wanting to do the right thing. But what is the right thing here? 'Who are these people?' I ask. 'Why are you removing them against their will? Are they criminals?'

'No, just illegal immigrants, nothing to worry about.' He smiles again. It's hard to concentrate on what he's saying over the man's screams.

'But why don't they want to go back? Are they going to be in danger in their home country?'

'No, of course not.' Another smile. 'Please have a seat, miss. We need to take off.'

He leaves and I sit down, worried now that we're attracting too much attention to ourselves. Do I really need any more trouble at this point? If I try to intervene on behalf of these people, I could be kicked off the flight. What would that accomplish? I don't know what to do.

The shouting continues. 'I don't want to go back, don't make me, you can't make me go back. Aaaaaah! Stop breaking my arm! Somebody help me...!'

The Australian says, 'Well, this flight's not going to be much fun, is it?'

His neighbour chuckles and cracks another joke.

A fat woman a few rows down is arguing with the stewardess to be moved away from all the noise. 'I paid to be on this flight, I refuse to travel under these conditions, upgrade me to a seat away from this ruckus!'

'I'm really sorry, madam, but the plane is full.'

As the plane takes off DeAnn is subdued and pensive, and she keeps fiddling with the plaster on her forehead. I asked her what happened yesterday but she won't say.

Colonel Groebler's arms are crossed, his legs sticking out into the emergency aisle and he looks asleep behind the dark, smoky glass of his iBubble. I've never seen one so opaque; it looks vaguely sinister, as if he'd been made prisoner and his head had been forced into a black hood.

Anthony is reading something so I look at the other passengers; the NGO woman is still absorbed in her dictation, assiduously ignoring everyone. The deportee keeps shouting, but his voice is hoarse now, and, to my shame, a part of me is annoyed with him. Surely, he realises that no one will do anything to help him?

Somewhere nearby but out of sight, a baby's crying his heart out, his screams mixing with the deportees' pleas in an unbearable concert. Poor kid. What have we done to his world?

And how on earth has the responsibility to save us all from this future fallen on my shoulders? I have no idea what I'm doing. I'm not qualified, I'm on my own and the Programme wants me dead.

Jesus Mary Joseph, how am I going to get out of this mess? Let alone save the planet? The plane lifts off the ground, as gravity tries to pull me back down, and for the first time, as I struggle to lift my head up and fail, I realise that I'm trapped by forces too big for me to control and that I might not make it back to 2016 alive.

ALSO BY O. M. FAURE

Olivia and DeAnn's story continues in the next book of *The Beautiful Ones* Trilogy: *Torn*.

THE CASSANDRA PROGRAMME SERIES:

The Disappearance (prequel)

THE BEAUTIFUL ONES (TRILOGY):

Book 1: *Chosen*

Book 2: *Torn*

Book 3: *United*

If you enjoyed *Chosen*, then you will love *The Disappearance*, the action-packed prequel that explains how the Time Travel Programme got started.

Grab your FREE copy of *The Disappearance* today simply by visiting www.omfaure.com!

BIBLIOGRAPHY

This book is based on scientific studies, UN forecasts and real data. If you would like to know more, please consult the sources listed below.

A list of book club topics to discuss is also available when you join the Readers' Club at www.omfaure.com

Overpopulation Analysis:
 • Cafaro, P. and Crist, E., Life on the Brink: Environmentalists Confront Overpopulation, Athens, Georgia: The University of Georgia Press, 2012.
 • Ehrlich, P., The Population Bomb, New York: Ballantine Books, 1971.
 • Emmott S. 'Humans: the real threat to life on earth', Guardian, 29 June 2013.
 • Furness, H., 'Sir David Attenborough: If we do not control population, the natural world will', Telegraph, 18 September 2013.
 • Jowit, Juliette, 'Three's a crowd', Guardian, 11 November 2007.
 • Meikle, J., 'Sir David Attenborough warns about large

families and predicts things will only get worse', Guardian, 10 September 2013.
  • Remarque Koutonin, M., 'Isn't it Europe that is over-populated rather than Africa?', Guardian, 11 January 2016.
  • Roberts, D., 'I'm an environmental journalist, but I never write about overpopulation. Here's why.' Vox, 29 November 2018
  • Bloom, D., 'Demographic Upheaval.', Finance and Development, a quarterly publication of the International Monetary Fund, March 2016.

UN Forecasts on Population:
  • United Nations, Department of Economic and Social Affairs, Population Division, 'World Population Prospects: The 2015 Revision'.

John B. Calhoun's Mice Utopia Experiments
  • Calhoun, John B., MD. 'Death squared: the explosive growth and demise of a mouse population', NCBI, January 1973.
  • Calhoun, John B., MD, Environment and Population: Problems of Adaptation: An Experimental Book Integrating Statements by 162 Contributors, Santa Barbara, CA: Praeger, 1983.
  • Fessenden, M., 'How 1960s mouse utopias led to grim predictions for future of humanity', Smithsonian.com, 26 February 2015.

Food and Water Scarcity:
  • Lederer, E. M., '20 million people in four countries facing starvation, famine: UN', The Associated Press, 10 March 2017.

• Menker, S., 'A global food crisis may be less than a decade away', TED Talk, August 2017.

• Wiebeɪ, K., Lotze-Campen, H., Sands, R., Tabeau, A., van der Mensbrugghe, D., Biewald, A., Bodirsky, B., Islam, S., Kavallari, A., Mason-D'Croz, D., 'Climate change impacts on agriculture in 2050 under a range of plausible socioeconomic and emissions scenarios', IOP Science 25 August 2015.

Bee extinction:

• Sarich, C., 'List of foods we will lose if we don't save the bees', Natural Society, 2 August 2013.

ACKNOWLEDGMENTS

This book exists thanks to so many people who have supported me, lifted me up and taught me along the way.

I owe so much to my godfather Alastair Pugh, who was an endless source of encouragements and hugs. I miss him already.

I particularly want to thank Lisa Handley, Marc Laurenson, Tony King and Nina Vox for guiding me onto my path.

I would not be who I am today without my mother's inspiring example and her unshakable faith in me.

I learned about Scenario planning a long long time ago in a country far far away and I'll always be indebted to Charles Thomas for showing me the future(s).

I'm so grateful to my fantastic manager, Jessica Magnusson for supporting me and giving me the time I needed to write.

And finally I want to thank Brittany Ganguly, Joan Diamond, Paul Ehrlich and the MAHB for their endorsement and encouragement.

ABOUT THE AUTHOR

 O. M. Faure studied political science at Sciences Po in Paris, before obtaining a Master's degree in International Affairs at The Fletcher School of Law and Diplomacy in Boston.

She has worked at the United Nations in Geneva and has extensive experience as a change and transformation manager in several banks over the last twenty years.

Today, she is a Principal at a Scenario Planning consulting firm, and she lectures and coaches at the Hult International Business School.

Based in London, O. M. Faure is a feminist, a Third Culture Kid, an enthusiastic singer, and a budding activist.

 facebook.com/omfaure
twitter.com/OM_Faure

Printed in Great Britain
by Amazon